S. L. Coe

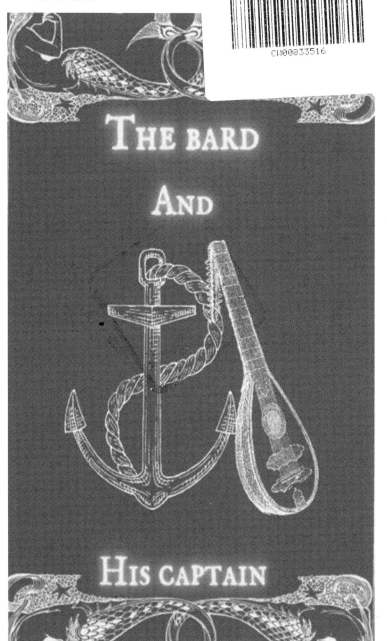

THE BARD

AND

HIS CAPTAIN

S. L. Coe

Copyright:

Damn Those Inkpot Gods by S. L. Coe

Published by Amazon KDP

www.literaturebyslcoe.com

Cover and title pages created via Canva by S. L. Coe

Map created via Inkarnate pro by S. L. Coe

ISBN: 9798833263181

Acknowledgements:

It would not be fair to begin this book without first acknowledging everyone who made this book a reality, and so without further ado I would like to say a huge, huge thank you to Briony J Shutt for supporting me throughout the entire writing process and allowing me not only to bounce ideas off of her, but also bombard her with random questions, without this wonderful woman and fellow author, my book would not exist.

I would also like to say a massive thank you to Iris, Erika and Marie for supporting my writing career and listening to me rant and rave about what my characters are currently doing, even if they haven't had the chance to read my work. And lastly, as always, I would like to say a huge thank you to my family for always standing by my side through thick and thin.

Dedications:

To,

Joey Batey, Madeline Hyland and the Amazing Devil, thank you for inspiring me to write this book, if it were not for the release of your album Ruin (as well as Horror And The Wild and Love Run) I fear I would not have had the inspiration to even outline the novel let a known write it.

And to you my reader,

Who at times believed that living in a fantasy universe would be much better than our real one, I agree, and so I hope you find solace in this book and my characters. Enjoy the adventure and allow yourself to run free in the land of fantasy.

Yours truly,
S. L. Coe

The Bard and His Captain book 1: Damn Those Gods
Inkpot

Damn those Inkpot

Gods

By S. L. Coe

Chapter 1: Oh you traitorous child.

"Stop! Stop...stop! Please. I'm begging you, leave her be!" Julian screamed as he tried to wrench his hands away from the mast, his eyes transfixed on the Captain who was stripped bare from the waist up. He watched unwillingly as the whip came slashing down over the Captains back.

And yet, she stayed silent and gritted her teeth as hot tears rolled down her cheeks. His back ached from his previous ninety-eight lashings, but his heart was heavier.

"God dammit, you sad sacks of shit, Listen to me! She is pregnant. For Christ sakes do not end two lives for the sake of one. If you must punish someone, then let it be me. I shall take half of her lashings and double of mine, if it means you will leave her be!" He pled as he fought to keep the growl at bay. He knew he was lying through his teeth, but by the gods, he couldn't care less. It was one thing to punish him for being an Elf, but it was another to drag the Captain away from her ship, merely because she had tried to help him. His blood boiled from within as he fought to free himself from the shackles.

"Oh, does the bard ever shut up?" the one-eyed torturer spat as he dragged the whip along the splintered deck of the ship and deliberately cracked it so that it flicked and curled around the bard's fingers.

"He does when you finally listen," Julian spat through gritted teeth, his eyes glistening with unrivalled anger. "What? You can hit a woman without mercy, but an Elf is what you're scared of? That's beyond pathetic-"

But before Julian could get another word out the whip crashed down upon his weeping back and clipped his ears. He stifled a whimper and glared at his torturer with a steely resolve. "Let her go, she played no part in this."

"Oh, and how are you so certain?"

"Because, I was at the tavern when she wandered in. Hell, her crew were drunk out of their skulls and almost ruined my set. I'm lucky that I know the tavern owner or else my career would have been ruined before it had barely begun."

"Fine. Send her to the brig, I'll deal with her tonight. As for the bard, we're going to have fun with you".

"Oh great..." Julian muttered beneath his breath. He kept his head down as he watched the Captain be hauled to her feet and dragged below deck. His heart ached to see her so vulnerable.

Down came the whip and slashed against his wet shoulder blades. His blood ran down his back and fell to the floor, and it was in times like these he cursed his Elven heritage, for his blood came out black. "Tell me everything you know about the captain."

"I barely know her- ah- what good do you think a
lashing is going to do? Are you that uncivilised that you
think violence is a better solution than asking a simple
question?" he cried as he tried to arch his back away
from the leather cane.

His efforts to avoid the whip were futile, as the torturer
grew impatient with Julian and thus unleashed his fury
on the poor bard's back. His legs buckled as he fought
to keep his body upright and he fell face first into the
mast. His chestnut waves stuck to his face, shielding his
eyes from view. With a great sigh he looked up to the
sky and muttered. "Enough...I'll talk."

"It took you long enough," the torturer chuckled
darkly as he struck the bard thrice more before finally
untying him.

Julian's legs were weak as he stood and readied himself
for the next blow. But it never came. The other
gentleman seated himself on a barrel and stroked the
whip as if it were a rabid dog that he had managed to
finally tame. Julian couldn't help but laugh as he
watched and waited for the other man to begin his
interrogation.

"What's so funny Bard?"

"Aside from your stupidity, the fact you are just sat
there doing fuck all, where did your bravado go?" he
said as he kept his back to the mast in order to try and
hide the fact he was using what little was left of his
magic to heal himself.

"Oh you traitorous child, just you wait until I get my hands on you," the torturer growled as he stood from the barrel and shoved it backwards. He ran towards Julian, who through his quick wit managed to duck beneath the older gentleman's legs and run along the starboard side of the ship, coming to an abrupt stop right in front of the captains' quarters.

"Ah, ah, ah, you wouldn't want to cripple a bard now would you? I could write songs that would have your name strewn throughout of all the taverns in west Draconda. They'd despise you, and besides would you really want to be seen punishing a prisoner in front of the captains living quarters? You know a captain awoken early, always leads to a bad day of travel," Julian rambled on, his back flush against the wall with only the broken backside of his lute left for him to wield.

"Funny you should say that; a beating is just what the captain ordered," the torturer glowered as he cracked the whip along the harsh sodden floor, his teeth - though rotten – glinting under the moonlight as he drew closer and closer to Julian.

"Oh fuck," Julian muttered, as he squeezed his eyes shut, gritted his teeth and allowed for the relentless beating to begin.

Chapter 2: The dastardly Bard and the

lonely captain.

Midnight was rapidly approaching as Julian stumbled between the guards. They marched him below the bowels of the ship and tossed him onto the frigid sodden floor of the aging cell. Julian hissed through the pain and threw a long string of curses back at the guards. But it was futile, for they were long gone and unable to hear his profanity, and if they did hear, they simply didn't care.

He tried to push himself to his feet before crumbling to the floor. Gritting his teeth, the skin on his hands felt as though they were burning from the inside out. The binding had dug far deeper than he had originally thought and his fingertips were cut and bruised from where he had tried to defend himself from the lashings. Another hissed elven curse slipped through his lips as he tried to heal the weeping wound on his back, and yet, his magic failed him.

♩ *"I fell onto a pirate ship.*

Lonely and lost,

Still at war with the rotten frost.

But now...

I'm left in a cell to rot,

They're all bloody useless,

The whole ruddy lot" 🎼

Julian muttered in an attempt to follow a tune, but his song fell on deaf ears and faded out into nothingness as the world around him seemed to grow darker and darker with every passing minute. Far too quiet for comfort, or that was until the captain pushed her hand through the bars of her cell and found the bards hand.

She tapped it twice before speaking in a hushed whisper, "Hey...er, Ju- Bard?...I'm sorry I never caught your name. But are you okay?"

He barely moved his head from where it hung between his knees, for the world never seemed to stop spinning as he watched the guards feet pace back and forth outside of their cell. "My condolences, love. I never caught yours either, but I am Julian Scott – the best bard of west Draconda or so I'm told," he introduced himself with a flourish of his hand, before muttering underneath his breath "although if my last song was anything to go by, I may well be a sham."

"Well if it's any consolation, I thought your voice was rather sweet albeit tainted." She chuckled as she shuffled around so that she was sat crossed legged across from him.

"Tainted?" he questioned, bemused and entertained as he lifted his head to get a good look at the captain before him.

"Well...let's just say, you certainly have a certain charm about you – and your accent is it...Elven?" she said as she ran her hands through her hair and thought of a way to keep him awake – for, she had seen many a man beaten by the whip succumb to death because they rested far too soon.

"Yes ma'am, I'm afraid your chamber mate is of Elfish blood," he said as he lifted his hair away from his ears, and let the stitches show. "I understand, if you would like to end our conversation."

"Good sir, what kind of captain do you take me for? I have many sailors all from different backgrounds and circumstances. My ship is their willing refuge. Besides that, you saved my life. And for that, I am forever in your debt."

"I believe it is the other way round. If you didn't save me from those bandits I would most certainly be left underneath an unmarked grave with my lute chucked into Kastilla's backwater river."

"Well then I guess we are equal," the captain smiled gently as she tried to figure out how big the cell was. "But what will come of you when you're finally free of this place?"

"Assuming they don't kill me," Julian swallowed and cleared his throat before continuing, "I will probably return to the tavern and hope to find myself in the elven kingdom that resides on Pixie Isle. "

"Wait, you don't mean the kingdom that is protected by devils and pixies alike, do you?"

"You know of the kingdom?"

"Of course! That's where I spent the majority of my youth before I found the Black Bess in the harbour a few years later." She beamed as she recalled the way the sun would greet her with its gentle rays and encourage her closer to the entrance despite knowing full well she could never be allowed to enter.

"My good lady, I know a man must never ask a lady her age, but I have the faintest feeling that I know you," he explained as he watched the moonlight drape of the captains golden skin and dance across her honey brown eyes before finally falling on her amber locks, "Did you ever wander the forest?"

"I did...come closer," she offered her hand through the bars as she moved her head away from the moonlight, fearing the full moon was nigh.

He did as he was told and shuffled closer. He raised a curious eyebrow as he felt her move his hair from in front of his forehead. "Is there something on my face?"

She quietly shushed him for a second as she held her hand over the rather large gash that resided on his eyebrow, which had been steadily weeping since he was thrown in the cell. She knew that by offering him her healing, she would lose years of her life. But she cared not, for in all of her 24 years of existence she had finally found someone who matched her, both in circumstance and wit. "There, it shouldn't scar too much."

"My lady, your hand...it's become skeletal," he said with wide eyes as he took her hand, holding it up to the moonlight. In doing so, the bones in her hand became more evident.

She shook her head and yanked her hand away from the moonlight. "It's nothing. Really," she insisted and closed her eyes in shame.

"Captain, there's nothing to be ashamed of. I'm sorry if my reaction had told you otherwise, it's just I have never seen a condition such as yours in real life before," he explained, moving back to sit with his back pressed to the cold wood of the ship.

"Sail with me," she suddenly demanded.

"I'm sorry, what?"

"Sail with me. I understand that you barely know me, and thus I understand if you deem me untrustworthy, but I think that we could help each other."

Julian paused for a moment as he thought about what the future could hold, about where his tales may take him, and what the captain could bring to him. "How so?" he questioned, taking great consideration in the wording of his question.

"You wish to gain access to the kingdom, correct?" she questioned, without waiting for his answer she continued. "And I require your help to find a cure to my condition, and you are the only one who knows about it – both in the now and the past. And so, if you sail with me, I will provide you with protection and shelter – and in exchange, you could help me find the cure".

"My lady there's n-" he began but stopped himself short for he feared losing her trust, and the position she could grant him, "Alright, I shall take you up on your offer. On one condition"

"Name it, anything you want, it's yours."

"You owe me a new lute," he said as he held his hand out for her to shake.

She looked at it once before her eyes trailed up his body and landed on his eyes, and she was met with nothing but genuine truth and trust. And with that, she took his hand and shook it firmly "Welcome aboard the Black Bess, Julian."

"Pleasure to be aboard, Captain Embers," he winked and laid down facing the ceiling. "We shall discuss plans in the morning, I assume?"

"Indeed we shall, good night Bard," she said through a yawn as she settled down on her side and closed her eyes, far beyond ready for the night to take her.

"Goodnight Captain," he chuckled and closed his eyes too. "May the dawn greet you with kindness."

"And let the night be full of kind dreams."

"As you wish," he muttered before falling into sleeps tender embrace.

Chapter 3: The hopeful morning gone to hell.

The dawn was steadily approaching as the ocean waves lapped at the side of the ship and seeped into the cells.

Julian gasped as the cold saltwater rose and slapped his face. "Oh god, Captain!" he cried out as he watched the water rise and struggled to climb away from it. But he was met with pure silence. "Come on captain, wake up! Lest you want to drown"

"One step ahead of you bard," she said as she clambered down the stairs and jangled the keys in front of him.

"How the hell did you get a hold of those?" he questioned as he attempted to rid himself of his shirt as it kept catching on the rust that lingered on the metal bars of his cell.

"A woman has to have some secrets," she quipped back with a wink before bouncing through the water and over to the lock. Her eyes stared transfixed on the bards lean chest as the keys shook in her hand. "Do you have a weapon?"

"I do not. Do you?"

"I have a spare dagger in my boot. Hold on," she said as she let the lock go and put her hand down the side of her knee high boots in an effort to find the dagger.

When she pulled it out, it glinted red in the sunlight.
"Here, catch!"

"Woah! Captain, I do not mean to undermine your
authority nor your jail break attempt, but throwing
daggers? You're lucky I have good hand eye
coordination," he said as he followed the path of the
dagger and caught the hilt before it hit the ground. His
chestnut brown curls flopped unceremoniously around
his temple as he bowed before standing and striding
over to the cell door. His hands found hers and guided
them to the lock. "Breathe, my captain. The chaos can
wait for us," he spoke softly as he looked down at her.

"It's not the chaos I'm worried about," she muttered as
they worked together to unlock the gate.

"Then what is it?"

"We don't have time to discuss it now," The Captain
stated as she pulled the keys from the gate and made a
watery dash for the stairs.

"Captain!" he shouted after her as he awkwardly
manoeuvred his way through the gate and ran after
her, but she ignored her title and kept climbing.
"Captain Embers! Listen to me! I may have only
known you for a day, but if I am to sail with you then
learn to lean on me. Let me shoulder your burden as I
did your lashings."

"Julian." She warned, her voice low and dangerous,
but as she turned to face him her eyes told a different
story. "You must understand, what we are about to

face may change your opinion of me, and for that I am sorry. But before you wish to trust me then you must let us experience this. And if the sentiment remains, then and only then, shall I divulge into what I have kept from you. Do we have a deal?" she questioned as she held her hand out for him.

"Fuck it, it can't be worse than what we saw last night," he said and shook her hand with a great might and a nod of respect before the two of them clambered up the stairs.

With one final look towards him she said, "That I wouldn't be so sure of. Ready yourself."

And ready himself he did, with his dagger in hand, his heart set on survival and the captains safety, he was ready to head fist first into battle.

***

The ships floor was ladened with bodies. The woods surface ran red as swords clashed and grated against metal, skin and wood. The cries of the enemy crew could be heard for miles, and Julian's blood ran cold as he watched the battle unfold before him. The dagger he held in his hand shook, and he turned to the captain, eyes wide and mouth agape. "Did you know this was happening?"

She looked back at him ever so slightly sheepish, and yet before any words could leave her mouth a sword swung down between them and a grotesque orc of 8 foot with muscles that seemed as though they would burst if they got any bigger stood before them. His voice boomed as he bent over to look down at the two companions who were successfully failing to escape his gaze. "Well, well, well, what do we have here then? Two straggly stowaways on my ship!"

And with the loud boom of the orcs voice, his crew turned to look at them, intrigued and ready to kill.

They all stalked towards them agonizingly slow, the dagger was beginning to slip from Julian's grasp as a cold shiver ran up his spine.

His gaze drifted from the crew to the captain as he drew in a breath of courage and grabbed the captains hand.

"Do you trust me?" he said with a fierce determination and began to edge them towards the starboard side of the ship as he knew the water would be deeper.

She followed his lead as they ducked under the swing of swords and narrowly avoided the arrows that were sent down from the mast. As he got one leg over the side of the ship a dagger came whizzing towards him and embedded itself within his side. He cursed under his breath and immediately clenched his hand around the weeping wound and tried to adjust the fabric of his trousers so that the majority of the blade would be hidden from the captains sight.

"Wait!" she called out as she threw her leg over the side, "Do you have any clue as to where we're going?"

"Gods no, I can get us to Pixie Isle-" he tried to explain as he gripped the wood in front of him for support, but his words died on his tongue as the arrow came for the captains head and he dove towards her. He wrapped his arms around her and with all of his might nudged them off of the ship and down into the deep waters below.

The world around them seemed to fade as the sea got darker and darker until no light shined through. His blood flowed freely in the unknown waters, and the creatures that lurked below seemed to grow in size and number as they swam towards him. He cursed under his breath and shook the captain who laid still in his arms, but when he got no response he knew then something was wrong.

He had to get to the surface.

He had to save the captain, even if it killed him.

And with that dagger in his side, he was damn sure it might.

***

Julian looked to the sky and thanked the gods that the shore was closer to him than he initially thought as he struggled to carry the captain to the sand and keep his blood from dripping onto her. His legs gave out and he fell towards the soft warm sand that resided on most of west Draconda's sea coasts. He cradled her head as he fell and took most of the force. Her breathing started to even out but her eyes remained unopened. "Captain, can you hear me?" he questioned as he placed his hands on both shoulders and gently shook her.

"You're very loud," she coughed and spluttered as she turned her face away from him. Her soft burgundy hair

fell around her like gentle waves, and her amber eyes
shinned like pools of gold as she looked up at him.

"And you gave me a fright and half," he said as he
brushed a stray strand of her out of her face before
untangling himself from her.

She froze under his touch and her cheeks seemed to
redden.

"Did I do something wrong?" he enquired as he tilted
his head to the side.

"I...no...not at all. You did everything right." She
stammered as she shook the more impure thoughts
from her mind, and went to stand, but found her legs
to be far more wobbly on sand than they ever have
been on sea.

"Woah there Captain, I know you want to get back to your ship but maybe we should take it easy for a while," he said as he stood - adjusted his trousers to hide the dagger - and held out his hand for the captain.

Which she took, much to his surprise, with great enthusiasm as she allowed herself to be hauled to her feet.

"I said you would need to learn to lean on me," he quipped almost playfully and began to lead the way to Pixie Isle.

"Oh shut up," she laughed as she shook her head and followed him down onto the winding path that was slowly being covered by trees and mystical sunlight.

Chapter 4: A sun filled tavern and a questionable crew.

Pixie Isle. It was everything and more as the fireflies danced through their air and allowed their wings to catch the sunlight and thus doing so cast beautiful colours on the ground that would have put stained glass to shame. The crows seemed to sing as Julian lead the way to a nearby lake, and whilst it was the height of summer, he knew the waters here were always cool and held healing properties even he didn't understand. It wasn't until he was at the water's edge – ready to strip into his small clothes – did he realise that his once cream shirt had now turned a rather intriguing shade of burgundy and the dagger was practically falling out of him. The back of his eyes pricked with unshed tears as he felt the dagger slice against his newly brandished B that stood as a reminder of the betrayal to his guild – a small price to pay for the freedom of Elves.

S. L. Coe

"Bard are you bleeding?" the captain enquired as she followed the trail of burgundy – black blood from where he stood several moments ago to the edge of the water.

"Please Captain, do not worry yourself with my mortal wounds," he said as he moved his arms out of the damp sleeves and held his hand up to her. In his peripheral vision he could see the captains hands glowing golden as they usually did when she was about to heal someone. "And do not waste your years on an injury I can sew together."

"Then what do you want me to do?" she asked as she undid her over- skirt and began to unlace her trousers.

"Join me in the lake, bathe, and be swift in pulling the dagger out," he said as he inhaled sharply and rid himself of his shirt and trousers until all he stood in

was his small clothes, which left a fair bit to the
imagination.

"Are you sure you trust me enough to pull it out?" she
questioned as she tossed her shirt over to the trees and
breathed a sigh of relief at the fact her undershirt was
still intact. She soon joined him in the lake and
shuddered a gasp at how cool the water was.

"I do. Now, please...it's getting rather painful," he
confessed as he looked up at her with a grimace.

"Alright, hold still," she nodded as she placed one
hand on his hip and selfishly allowed for her fingertips
to linger before her other hand found the handle of
the dagger. At that moment he could have sworn he
could die happy as he touch caused sparks to fire
within him and the muscle on his abdomen to twitch
and flex, out of fear and perhaps a small amount of
romantic intrigue. Or that was until the captain took

the moments distraction to rip the dagger out of him in one through sweep that left his lungs breathless and his legs weak as he stumbled forward towards the captain. He muttered an apology under his breath as she just managed to catch him.

"Now whose leaning on who," she chuckled as she gently pushed him down to sit on the lakes bank. "But I do apologise for how roughly I pulled."

"Nonsense, it was rather efficient," he barked a husky laugh. "Ow! Okay laughing is definitely off of the table," he groaned as he fingered the wound and tried to determine the depth.

"Do you think the fae will allow us to ask them for a sewing kit?"

"How do you know about the fae?"

"My ship is manned by a few, and there is always a strange, sweet smell in the air when they are about," she explained as she gestured to the side of the tree that bathed in sunlight, and in that sunlight laid the sprites that the fae used to travel in when they did not wish to be in their humanoid form. "See?"

"You become more and more intriguing by the hour, my lady," he said as he smiled proudly at her, before leaning back on the bank and pushing the water so it lingered over his thigh. "But to answer your question, I fear they may ask for something in return. A name for instance."

"It's okay, I have a plethora of enemy names to choose from," she said as she patted his thigh and stood to walk to the sunlight. "My darling fae, might I exchange a name for a few medical supplies such as a sewing kit?" she enquired as she crouched down and spoke in an elevated happy manner in order to gain their favour. Which indeed they gave with a few musical notes and flew off in a hurry and promised to bring it to the lake.

 "Thank you Captain," he said softly as he kept applying pressure to the wound, whilst his eyes laid transfixed on hers.

"You are most welcome, my bard," she smiled softly as she brushed his hand away from the wound to get a closer look.

But in doing so, he caught her wrist, and his eyes flickered from her wrist to her lips to her eyes, and hers mirrored his. "Darling Captain, what did I say about using your magic?"

"I'm not going to use magic. I was going to check your wound and make sure you laid down flat so the wound remains accessible. Will you do that for me or will I have to force you?" she said as she allowed her fingers

to splay gently over his before pulling her hand free

and looking at him with a raised eyebrow.

"Well, I guess you're just going to have to force me,"

he quipped back with a challenging gaze of his own

and shuffled so that his bottom half was submerged in

water and his top half was lingering on the lake bank.

Ever so close to laying down.

"If that is your wish, then I guess as Captain, I must

comply," she smirked playfully and in one swift

motion, grasped his wrists, pushing them above his

head, and in doing so pinning him to the bank just as

several sprites flew to her side with the sewing kit in

hand. "Ah thank you, my darling fae. And for

payment, my name is: Luci Jester."

And with that the fae deposited the sewing kit in her

hands and buzzed close to Julian's reddened face with

elven murmurs of: "Good luck there Julian. Have fun and stay safe," before they danced into the distance in hopes of finding themselves in the nearby tavern.

"Well, you are certainly more bold than I first thought you would be," he rambled as he looked everywhere bar at her in hopes that his blush would go away just as quick as it appeared.

"There's a lot about me you don't know," she said as she placed her hand over the wound and brushed all the flaking moss and skin away from it, before threading the needle and beginning to thread it threw his skin. The needle was like fire as it tore through his porcelain skin and began to bring his skin together.

"We have a lot of time," he hissed through gritted teeth. "And I for one, would like to get to know you better."

"As I would you...did...did you betray your guild?" she

said as her hand brushed against the rather large,

branded B that stood as a reminder for his betrayal,

which saved thousands of elven lives.

"I did, and it wasn't a decision I made lightly, believe

me. But at the end of the day, it was my life or the

thousands of lives that belonged to the elves and fae

that live along the coast of Tortoya. And it only made

sense to save them from slaughter and more torture,

even if it did cost me the tops of my ears and my

courtly reputation," he sighed as he finally met her

eyes and tried to keep from cursing out in pain.

Her eyes were soft and understanding as she listened

to his explanation and said nothing but offered a quiet

understanding. She moved herself so that she was

hovering over his lap and reached across for more

thread and a wider needle to gather the deeper layers

of skin.

"But what about you, why do you not trust your crew?" he said as he wriggled his fingers to keep his mind distracted from the captain who looked as though she was the epitome of perfection as her burgundy hair seemed to glow in the sunlight, and the amber of her eyes shined bright as she looked down at him, intrigued and focused.

"You stare an awful lot, did you know?" she said as she brushed his damp sweaty hair from his forehead, her gaze and touch lingering on his soft face and sharp jaw bones.

"You're a fine one to talk," he quipped back, "But you are avoiding my question, forgive me if I have overstepped the mark, but I just wanted to know how you felt about the crew before we step back onto your ship."

"You haven't overstepped the mark; I just wasn't
expecting you to approach the question with such
confidence. Although that said, you are a bard...so it
makes sense," she cleared her throat before finishing
the last few stitches and encouraging him to lower
himself into the lake to finish the healing process. He
quickly followed her command and sat by her side as
he allowed the summer sun to kiss them both. "Sorry
I'm rambling, but if you must know, I do trust my
crew...for the most part."

"For the most part, are there any members of your
crew that put you on edge?"

"In the past, there most certainly has been a select few
members of crew that decided to organise a mutiny
against me, and when it went tits up on their end due
to the other half of the crew defending me...let's just
say the end result wasn't pretty," she said as she
indicated to her scar that resided across the bridge of

her nose. "He would have had my eye if the rest of the crew hadn't stepped in."

"Then why didn't you abandon him at the next port?"

"Because he was the only man who knew how to man the crew when I wasn't there."

"Even so, he does not deserve to sail with you. Especially not after that. But what about the rest of the crew?"

"The rest bar the cannon masters, are wonderful. They're the closest thing to family I have," she said sadly, as she ran her hand through the water, accidentally grazing his thigh, and gave him a small apology. To which he simply shook his head and said there was no need to apologize.

"I'm sure they feel the same about you Captain, after all, already in the small amount of time I've known you, you've already made me feel at home," he said as he stood from the lake and walked to the bank ready to climb out and redress.

"Thank you!" she called out as she swept her captains hat up from the tree and placed it on her head before proceeding to dress herself from bottom to top.

"For what?" he questioned as he looked over his shoulder at her, and met her eyes, hers filled with bewilderment, his with confusion.

"You saved my life; without you I would have been whipped till death took pity on me."

"But my darling Captain," he sighed lovingly as he turned around to face her, gently placing his fingers on her chin and tipping it ever so slightly so her gaze was distracted from the ground. "Without you, I would have drowned at sea – unknown, uncared for. But now I could write several lengthy ballads about the brave and resilient captain who saved me and may be winning over my lukewarm heart."

A faint blush dusted her cheeks as she listened to his words, and a soft smile danced across her lips. "Well, we best get you to a tavern then. Because I for one, cannot wait to hear the tale," she grinned and finished tying her over skirt before she took him by the hand and ran down the tree covered path.

"But I need a lute!" he called after her and ran to match her speed.

"And we'll find one, now come on, we need to get there before moonlight falls!"

❋ ❋ ❋
41

"It's three in the afternoon!"

"Tit for tat, Bard!"

"I'll give you tit for tat," he chuckled and took the lead as he lead them towards the sound of music, he couldn't help but smile at the sound of the villagers singing remnants of his old songs. "Come my lady, I know a shortcut."

***

The short cut itself was more of a long cut as they wandered down winding paths and stumbled in and out of trinket shops until all that was left was dust and their arms were full of stuff they didn't really need nor could they carry. But their pure giddiness that came from the calmness of Pixie Isle kept that curious spark alive, until they finally made it into the Locked box tavern, that was full to the brim with creatures that spanned anyway from dwarfs and halflings to regal elves and bawdy gentle orcs.

"OH MY GOSH! IT'S JULIAN SCOTT! HE'S REALLY HERE!" a young gentleman shrieked unceremoniously as he came bolstering over the tables and chairs before enveloping Julian in a large hug.

Julian's arms stayed where they were as he eyed the gentleman with a curious spooked gaze. "Sorry, I don't believe we've met," he muttered as he tried to keep everything within his arms and flashed a look that screamed help me to the Captain.

"I think you have yourself a fan," she whispered as she emerged from behind him.

"I can tell that, but why is he hugging me?" he

whispered back.

"You don't know who I am?" the younger gentleman

said as he finally let Julian go – although that wasn't

without a large sniff to gather Julian's unique smell of

apples, cinnamon, lute lacer, pine and fire.

"I'm afraid not," he said with a great effort not to

breathe a sigh of relief, "my arms are rather full at the

moment, would you mind if we were to continue this

conversation after I find a room for the two of us...as

in me and the captain," he said gesturing with his head

towards his new companion, just to drive the point

home that the younger gentleman's presence was not

welcome.

"If we must, then I shall wait by the hearth," he sighed

but reached out to Julian and caught his shirt, and with

a crooked grin plastered on his lips. "But Julian, be

S. L. Coe

sure to sleep with one eye open tonight, fate is not in your favour."

"Yeah...okay, we shall be going now," he said as he gently nudged the captain and as quickly as he could stalked over to the bar where the usual bar keep sat, polishing the tankards. "Oh good Anya you're still here."

"My gosh, you look spooked. Are you all right? It's not the hunters again is it?" Anya said as they leaned across the bar and untangled their hair from their antlers and went to grab a sword from behind the bar.

"No, it's not that. We need a room one with two beds, as soon as possible. I'm trying to hide from a fan and compose a song," he said as he nodded over towards the hearth where the young gentleman stood nursing a rather full tankard of ale with a menacing look in his eye and a set of parchment and ink in his hand. He caught Julian's eye and waved with a false smile, and

the bard cursed internally as he waved back and

returned his attention to the bar keep.

"I've never known you to hide from a fan before."

Anya explained as she looked through her key draw

and came up short, "As for the room...I regret to tell

you this, but I only have one room for tonight, and

there is only one bed."

"I can take the floor, you need the bed more than

me," Julian said quickly, not wanting to disappoint the

captain nor lose her favour.

"Are you sure? I don't mind taking the floor, I've slept

on plenty during my time on this earth."

"That I'm sure you have, but if this is the one night

you get to enjoy some little comfort then please, take

it," he said as Anya handed him the key and lead the two to their room.

"We could share the bed," she suggested, but Julian just shook his head at the idea – too stubborn to place aside his respect for her honour.

"I shall leave you two to it, but if you need anything, and I mean *anything,* I shall be downstairs so do not hesitate to let me know," she said with a wink in the pairs direction before wandering away with a soft mutter of 'destiny will entwine those two'.

Chapter 5: One bed and the enemy

"Thank you Anya" he chuckled and shook his head as he dismissed the wonderful tavern maid and turned to open the door that Anya had so kindly unlocked.

"Are you sure you don't wish to share a bed with me?" the captain asked as she marvelled at the small double bed that was pressed up against the hard oak wood, with just the smallest gap to hide ones gold or trinkets at the side. The golden covers were fringed with red lace and tucked neatly into the corners, albeit a little tighter than one would hope. The bright window stood open and allowed the dazzling sunlight to wash over the bed and it's later occupants.

"My darling captain, I cannot allow myself to defile your honour. I shall take the floor tonight and I will see if Anya has any spare blankets to keep you from growing cold during the night," he said as he placed

S. L. Coe

down his trinkets and began to lacer his lute as he sat himself on the wooden stool that sat in the far corner, just out of sight of the large window.

"At least let me buy you a tankard or two of ale to make up for it, and as a thanks for everything you've done for me thus far," she said as she sat crossed legged on the bed and watched as he paid close attention to the strings.

"I would like that milady; I think I have a few gold septum's in my coin purse that you can use to get yourself a round of drinks," he said as he nodded over to his small satchel that sat just below his large tomes.

"You're not going to join me?" she said as she heard him pluck a test-worthy note.

"I will, in time, but I need to compose my song before this evenings performance. And as much as I want you to be the first one to hear it, I don't wish to spoil the effect by you hearing me miss a note or flub a lyric. So please, enjoy your ale and talk to a few of the locals, and I shall meet you down there in an hours or twos time," he said as he ran his hands through his soft brown hair and scratched lightly at his beard before continuing to tune his new lute. "Oh and steer clear of that rat nosed man by the fire. I don't trust him."

"Neither do I," she admitted and began to slip off of the bed and head towards the door, "I do hope you'll join me for a drink later, bard."

"That I will. Now go! Enjoy yourself and I shall see you this evening, Miss Embers," he said with a gentle smile as he moved to the bed and encouraged her to leave and head downstairs.

"Okay, I'm going now. But I'll hold you to that!" she laughed as she grabbed her coin purse and slipped out of the door with a cheeky kiss blown towards the bard, who simply shook his head with an impressed smile.

As the door shut, Julian began to strum his lute in a 1, 2, 4, 3, 2 rhythm and allowed the lyrics to come to him as he danced around the room, just to get the bouncy rhythm and noise right.

♪

"I never gave much thought as to where the sunlit path could lead,

So many ships, so many avenues.

But there was only one that lead to you...~

Inkpot

The damp and cold, were nothing when you had eyes

of bold.

And a strength to hold your own against a crew of

50,000.

Her hair is stunning, filled with flecks of gold.

And of my heat, she has the

strongest hold,"

♪

he sang to himself as he strummed the lute, but soon
put it to the side as the rhythm fell flat on his well-
trained ears. And thus, he resulted to putting the lute a
side and digging under the bed for a piece of rough
parchment and some old lead.

"That's it I shall write her a ballad!" he cried and quickly got to work.

***

It was several hours later when Julian finally emerged from the room, with his hair tied back into a low ponytail, and his poet shirt unbuttoned dangerously low, he began to strum his lute in the strumming rhythm of 1,2,4,3,2, and swayed seductively down the stairs as he made his way onto the centre stage that steadily began to fill with a mages fog. And thus it allowed him to remain protected, whilst also improving his performance quality. Everyone in the tavern turned to watch him and guide the captain to the seat closest to the stage.

He took a swig of ale as he continued to strum the lute and hum the old Elven melody that many of his songs were based upon, but this time something was different.

For this song seemed cheerier with brief moments of seduction as he began the first verse which told in elvish a tale of a bard and his captain, who battled the dead and healed the wounds that resided on their heads – before dipping down into a swirl and coming to sit on the edge of the stage.

His eyes met hers across the smoke filled stage, as he picked up the familiar 1,2,4,3,2 rhythm and sang:

" **"I never gave much thought as to where the sunlit path could lead,**

So many ships, so many avenues.

But there was only one that led to you...~

* * *

The Silver and Gold are nothing to compare your eyes
so bold.

And a strength to hold your own against a crew of
50,000.

Her hair is stunning, filled with flecks of gold.

And of my heart, you my dear, have the strongest of
hold's.

But what was the question you bestowed upon me,

As we laid captive deep beneath the sea?

My darling Captain, would you sail with me?

With me, with you, with me...

With you, with me, with you,

Oh my darling Captain, would you sail with me? "

As he sang the last line, he reached out for the captains hand and placed a gentle kiss on her knuckles before giving it a light squeeze and sent her a wink before dancing his way through the crowd and back up to the stage. "My beautiful audience, you have been a pleasure to entertain, and once my hearts wishes have been fulfilled, I will return with a greater symphony," he beamed as he finished the last note of his song and bowed to the booming sound of clapping and cheers of encore.

And yet, despite his rising excitement and joy he knew something was off as the mages fog seemed to fade and through the crowd the shrewd younger gentleman slithered through the crowd and came to the edge of the stage, leant his elbows close to where Julian stood – and with a smarmy grin, cooed to him "Come on **Bard**, what's one more song?"

Julian's lip curled in disgust as he glared daggers at the younger gentleman who tainted his once favoured pet name, "Es aep Villianas, scrotden marga," he spat in Elvish, thankful that there was only a select few members of the audience who were fluent in Elvish, one of those being Anya.

Across the bar she'd watched the scene unfold, sword gripped at her side as she eyed the shrewd man and watched the way in which he reacted to Julian's performance. "ENOUGH! Apollo Tome, this is your final warning! Taunt the bard or his Captain again, and I will not hesitate to place your head on a spike and parade it around the town!" Anya boomed across the sound of the crowd and slammed the sword down on the counter just to show how serious she was about that.

And yet Apollo simply seemed to shrug his shoulders and shove away from the stage with a flourished bow towards Anya, and almost hissed "My apologies, it shan't happen again," before beckoning the bard to follow him.

"Liar," Julian spat as he jumped down from the stage, and B lined straight for the bar. He did not wish to have this conversation sober nor protected by Mages fog.

"Oh, so you do remember me," Apollo said as he slid into the space next to Julian, who internally groaned and turned his gaze to his large tankard of ale.

"No. I do not remember you in the slightest, so please enlighten me as to why you are so insistent on ruining not only my set, but my night," he said as he slammed the tankard back on the bar and shot Anya an apologetic glance, shifting his eyes over to the captain who stood against the pillar, toying with a dagger as she watched Apollo grate on everyone of Julian's last nerves.

"All will become clear in time, as for your captain, you ought to be wary of the midnight moon," he smirked, his teeth becoming more and more rat like by the minute, his eyes crinkled in the centre and his pupils turned into slits.

"What do you know about the Captain? Because I swear to you Mr. Tome, if you lay a single hand, nay a single finger on her, I will ensure you will never be able to do that again," he growled as he stepped into the younger gentleman with fire in his eyes, and the magic in his hands glowing red.

"That's for me to know and you to find out," Apollo

said smugly and began to turn away from Julian with a

pompous flaunt of his shoulders.

"Jashen danva!" Julian spat in Elven as he reached out

to grab Apollo's shoulder so that he would turn to face

him, and yet before he could the Captain stood before

him; eyes wide and shaking as she watched the magic

glow in his hand. The tavern fell silent as he dissipated

his magic and turned his face from her. His body

burned from the inside out as Apollo went to his usual

menacing corner by the hearth and began to write with

such a velocity the bard was half certain the charcoal

would break.

Julian sighed as his gaze lingered on the captain, "I'm

sorry my dear, I never intended for you to hear nor

see me behaving in such a vile and cruel manner. I will

answer all your questions, but first I need some air" he

said softly as he placed a gentle hand on the Captains

shoulder before placing several gold pieces and a note

on the bar for Anya, and then darting up the stairs and towards their shared bedroom.

The Captain stared after him and picked his lute up from where he'd left it on the stage, she looked between the bar and the stairs unsure of where to go. "Go after him, he might seem on edge tonight, but I think it would do well to talk to him. It's not often he runs into Apollo."

"I will, but Anya, who is Apollo and what the hell did Julian say in Elvish?" she questioned, well and truly bewildered.

"I didn't think it would be long before you asked that," she chuckled as she offered the captain a seat behind the bar, "The first thing he said 'Es aep Villianas, scrotden marga' essentially means 'you are a villainous bastard, of the highest class and the second thing he said 'Jashen danva' without a direct translation, roughly means 'traitorous liar'; our bard may be a wordsmith and a great performer when it comes to the English language, but when his fury gets the better of him, he often turns to Elvish insults," she explained as she shook her head and looked towards the stairs, where Julian sat at the top, unable to open the room due to a lack of key. "He means well, and he cares deeply for you."

"I know he does, and I...bur- care for him deeply too. But this, although I've only known him for a few days, was something different entirely. I didn't realise just how wonderful his performance was. He truly knows the way to a woman's heart," she said as she shot a soft gaze up to the stairs before returning her attention to Anya, who slipped the key to the captain.

"What did I say, destiny has plans for you two."

"Shush! We don't know that for certain and besides, the moon is nigh," she said as she took the key and slipped it underneath her hat.

"I know it is. Hence why I shall allow Julian to tell you what he will about the gentleman by the hearth. Go forth and sleep well."

"I shall, thank you Anya," she said and dashed towards the stairs and up them, as Julian moved towards the door – shame and self- disappointment littered all over his face.

"Are you sure you won't share the bed with me tonight?" she asked as she dug the key out from underneath her hat and unlocked the door for them. But he simply shook his head and took a pillow from beneath the bed as well as an additional blanket so that he could make a makeshift bed on the floor.

With a gentle sigh she locked the bedroom door and readjusted the cover and the bed so that it was out of sight of the moonlight.

***

Julian stared at the ceiling for what felt like hours, his body was freezing from the inside out as he clutched to the thin blanket. Despite the cold that brewed inside him, his heart thumped against his chest with worry, had he lost the captains favour? Did he mess everything up by cursing in elvish? Every negative questioning thought swam in his head, until the captain finally broke the silence with a shrill squeal.

"Captain! What's wrong?" Julian cried as he fought his way out of the blanket and to her side.

She laid with her hand over her mouth and pointed towards the ceiling "There's a massive spider dangling from the ceiling, I fear it might just bite me. Can you kill it?"

"A spider? I don't see anything," he said as he kneeled on the side of the bed and gazed up at the ceiling.

"It's on the centre beam, you'll have to stand on the bed to get it," she said as she shuffled over to the wall so that he could stand on the bed.

He raised a curious eyebrow at her, but followed her instructions, stood on the bed and searched for invisible spider, and yet as he thought he caught sight of the eight legged fiend, he felt a cold hand wrap around his ankle and pull him down with such a force that when he landed on the bed all the air he had kept in his lungs, escaped him.

He turned his head as he coughed and spluttered in an attempts to regain his breath, and it was only then did he realise that in his fall he had accidentally pushed the captain into the gap beside the wall. "My captain are you alright?" he gasped as he turned on his side and held a handout for her.

"I think I'm stuck," she laughed as she tried to grip onto the cover and haul herself up from the gap.

"Come, grab my hand and push yourself up," he laughed softly as he admired his futile attempts and wrapped his fingers on his right hand around her wrist and kept his thumb on her pulse, his cheeks flushed a light pink as he felt it speed up beneath his touch, and she mirrored him – completely.

"Ready?" she questioned as she placed one hand on the wall, and the other around his wrist.

S. L. Coe

"As I'll ever be," he agreed, and with that the two of them worked in partnership to pull her out of the gap, and yet, in doing so the cover came with them and wrapped the two of them in an awkward embrace. As limbs ended up in unfortunate places and hands were made to roam as they tried to find their bearings. "Well, hello to you too," he chuckled nervously as her face was inches away from his.

"Hi," she smiled and pushed herself up, only to slip back down as the headboard tilted towards them. "It appears we're stuck again."

"So it does," he said from beneath the covers. His gaze drifted from the ceiling to her amber eyes, and all the worry that was circulating his mind, seemed to subdue and disappear quicker with every passing second. "Captain Embers, can I ask you something without you believing I'm strange?"

"I make no promises, but please, ask away."

"Did I offend you this evening? I know my performance was very much tailored to you – but that was only because I wanted to thank you for everything you have done for me this far, and I wanted people to know about the wonderful captain who is steadily becoming my muse, and yet, I seem to have ruined it all by er...insulting Apollo in Elvish. It was not the first thing I wished for you to hear me say in my native tongue," he rambled on as they started to untangle themselves from the covers and lay side by side in the warm bed.

"Julian?" she spoke his name in a question and turned his head so that he was facing her.

"Yes Miss Embers?"

S. L. Coe

"Please stop worrying. It'll turn your luscious brown hair grey before it is time," she warned and met his gaze, showing him that with the words that were about to come, she was well and truly genuine. "You did not offend me, not even in the slightest, and as for your performance...it was truly breath-taking, I'm surprised you didn't hear me singing your praises to Anya. And as for the elvish insults, once I found out what they meant, they were actually quite entertaining, and I think it is rather endearing you leapt to my defence, even when I was not fully present."

"Well firstly thank you for singing my praises, I am truly pleased you liked my performance," he smiled softly as he moved the covers so that she was covered, whilst he laid on top of them "And I am glad I did not offend you. I promise you though I will write you a song in true elvish and if you like it, then I shall perform it every night. Oh, and I will tell you all I know about Apollo come morning light. That I owe you," he promised and turned on his side so that he could lean over the edge of the bed, and fiddle around

in his satchel of newly brought belongings. It wasn't

long before he finally found what he was after. "Here,

this is for you," he said as he presented her with a

small rectangular gold box.

"What is it?"

"Open it."

And open it she did with trembling hands, and inside

there laid a brand new pair of black lace gloves, that on

tips of the fingers – up to the second knuckle – and on

the cuff of the sleeve that resided just below her pulse,

laid several gold vines that sprouted off into fern

leaves. "How much did this cost you?"

S. L. Coe

"Price is not an issue. I knew the full moon was due, and I spotted these in the window of the glove makers and I just could not resist them. Do you like them?"

"Like them? Julian, they are the most beautiful item of clothing I have ever seen," she beamed as she slid them onto her small hands and admired the way the vines almost seemed to move with her.

"Thank you, oh and you should probably know that they are enchanted. With Elven and fae magic that is, so should the moons effects become too much for you to bear, these gloves should alleviate the pressure and lessen the effects."

"Julian, you must allow me to repay the favour when we get to pixie isle or aboard my ship," she said, full to the brim with giddy excitement.

"There is nothing to repay," he said as he offered her a

grateful smile, "we have a long day of travelling

tomorrow."

"That much I know."

"Then it is with that my captain, I must bid you

goodnight," he said as he went to move off of the bed

before she wrapped her arms around his waist and

pulled him back towards her.

"Stay with me tonight...please?" she questioned as she

pressed her face against his clothed back.

"But your honour-"

"Fuck my honour, I need to know you'll be safe

tonight and the only way I can do that successfully is if

you stay in my bed. So please, stay? I only ask this of you." She begged as he watched her with wide eyes and after several moments of hesitation, agreed.

"Shuffle over, my dear," he yawned softly and lifted the covers so that she could lay down comfortably and he placed a pillow beneath his head before joining her under the covers, unsure of what to do with his arms, he laid there still.

"Goodnight, my sweet, sweet bard."

"Goodnight, my darling Captain," he spoke softly and waited for her to be asleep and well before he too began to drift off until morning light.

Chapter 6: Breakfast, Tome, a map and a wayward journey.

The next morning came swiftly and with little hassle. Julian held several maps under one arm and cautiously balanced two bowls of boiling hot pottage on the other arm. He looked at it with a stiffened grimace. His hair remained perfectly dishevelled, as his curls brushed his cheeks and fell to his jaw whilst the rest of his hair sat in a short low ponytail at the nape of his neck. His shirt was absent, and his black breeches sat on his hips.

"Here eat this." He said as he placed the bowl of pottage in front of the Captain. "It'll probably taste as shit as it looks, but it will keep you full for the next four days, and with a journey like ours ahead, you will need your strength," he explained as he sat down opposite her, their legs brushed under the table, his right leg resided in between hers and his left resided on the outside. A blush dusted over both of their cheeks as they continued to nudge legs and share a meaningful gaze across the table.

"What is it?" the Captain asked as she lifted the spoon and eyed the contents with a disgusted curiosity as she watched it plop back into the bowl.

"It is intended to be pottage. It is a mix of oats, raisins, vegetables, meat and whatever was left over from last night's meal," he said as he forced down a mouthful of the foul meal. "Do you need some ale, or maybe some milk to wash it down?" he asked as he watched the captain struggle with the taste.

"I think that would be for the best," she chuckled awkwardly and attempted to eat again, "I don't mean to offend Anya, I'm sure she's a wonderful cook, but this is rather…"

"Strange?" Anya offered as she placed two silver jugs of milk on the table, "But you needn't worry, I take no offence. I'm surprised our bard can stomach it."

"It is not without struggle, my dear," he said as he poured milk into his tankard and pushed it towards the captain, before pouring another glass.

"That much I know," she chuckled before becoming deadly serious and turning her attention towards the maps that Julian had left at the end of the table. "But, in all seriousness, steer clear of the forest that leads to the Elven kingdom, so many of the kings guards reside there and they will not hesitate to kill you on sight."

"But I am the kings son," he whispered low enough that only Anya would be able to hear him.

"I know, but with your ears missing and him claiming to have no heir…it will not go as you plan" she whispered back and met his eyes, her own pleading with him "Please do not allow me to become an only child."

"Then come with us!" he said with bold confidence and pushed his bowl to the side whilst he unrolled the map and began to mark the map.

"And leave the tavern open for bandits and Tome? I cannot."

"Please Anya, I only want to gain entry to the kingdom, just once to show face, and then you can leave me be," he pleaded as Anya stood to return to the bar.

"I'm sorry Julian, but I cannot join you. I'm sure the Captain will be company enough," she said as she threw her hair behind her shoulders and returned to the bar.

Julian opened his mouth to speak, and yet, he found himself speechless and his eyes pricking with irritated tears. He wished for nothing more than to be home, to find himself accepted by the very society that he saved and they saw as little more than a bastardised outcast. But alas, that seemed impossible, or that was until the captain reached across and pulled his hand away from his face.

"Julian Scott, I swear to you one way or another, I will ensure you have a safe passage to the kingdom that you worked so hard to save. And I will see your entry and safety throughout your mission, that much I promise you. Captain's honour" she swore as she drew her initials in the air to sign the promise.

"And I will protect you from the moon, and no matter what it takes, I will find a cure to your moonlit curse" he said as he ran his finger over the top of her hand and signed his initials.

"Our fate is sealed" she said as she gave his hand a squeeze and finished the last of her pottage and drained the last of her milk.

"So it is, I deeply look forward to our endeavours" he smiled and took the empty crockery to the bar before heading upstairs to change into something more suited to travelling across rocky seas.

***

"Are you certain you will not come with me?" Julian questioned as he stood at the tavern door and fiddled with the leather lute strap that resided across his chest.

"Julian..." Anya began with a sigh, as she looked at the bard who with the morning sunlight behind him, looked like the spitting image of Elven royalty.

But alas, he held his hand up to stop her. "I know, the tavern" he explained with a knowing look and held his arms out for her – a welcoming embrace awaiting. "Please do not let the tavern come to harm, and should Apollo cause you any kind of harm, send a courier or a mage after me as soon as physically possible," he whispered into Anya's hair as he held her close.

"I would never dream of losing the tavern, not after everything you did to provide a safe haven. But brother mine, do not allow yourself to be bitten by the Vampires, not even to save the Captain." She warned as she let him go and moved aside to access the small cubby hole that resided behind the bookcase next to the front door.

"I think I know well enough by now that a Vampire's bite is truly fatal to an Elf."

"Maybe so, but that does not mean to say you won't jump in front of the captain to save her from their fangs."

He opened his mouth to say something but soon shut it again as he knew it would be futile to fight against the truth. And instead, he studied her as she clinked several bottles together as she pushed them out of the way and dug about the cubby hole to try and find the potion she was after.

"Here, take these. I stole them from Tome last night when he was drunk. I'm unsure of the effects, but the mage recons they are healing potions, and should reverse the effects of the vampire's poison, provided you catch it early enough," she explained as she reached for his satchel and placed the potions in deep behind his ink pot.

"Thank you." He said as he gave her hand a squeeze and waved the captain over, stepping further into the sunlight. "Keep yourself safe dear sister, I shall be back as soon as the second moon of May falls."

"I will hold you to that," she said as she watched the pair walk into the gentle sunlight and unto the dusty path that lead towards the southern end of Pixie Isle, and later the Elven kingdom.

"And I shall live up to your standard!" he called back as the wind ruffled through his emerald- green Elven cloak that was laden with Elven scripture underneath the hood. His cream cravat shirt served little purpose as he left it open until it reached just below his toned pectorals, in turn it allowed for his light brown chest hair to peak through. And with a gentle smile, he waved goodbye to his younger sister, and allowed his soft curls to blow widely in the wind.

S. L. Coe

"Keep him out of trouble!" Anya called out to the captain as they moved out of sight.

"I make no promises!" the Captain laughed as she pushed down her red over skirt to keep it from blowing up in the wind, and thus she had to keep a hand on her hat to keep it on her head and allow the wind to ruffle through her brown trousers and tight red bodice instead.

And with that, the Captain and the Bard set off to find the Elven kingdom.

Chapter 7: The Elven kingdom and the rejection of the bastard son.

The journey through the forest was tedious as every turn lead them back to the same old tree, to the same old route, and Julian's blood began to boil as he threw himself down on a half rotted tree stump and groaned when he half fell off it. "This is all his fault!" Julian spat as he gestured harshly in the direction of the castle that just a few days ago, he had profusely yearned to gain access to.

"Who's fault?" the captain enquired as she sat on the grass beside him and rested her head on her knees as she listened intently to his voice.

"My fathers," Julian said as he drew in a sharp breath, pressed his lips together and shook his heads as he looked up to the heavens before beginning to speak

S. L. Coe

again. "He knows that – despite my blood, and despite everything I've done – without my ears, to him, I am worse than human. I do not exist in his eyes. And thus, he has banished me from finding the castle."

"But you're still an elf! Surely your blood would lead you home, no?" she questioned with a determined fire in her eyes.

"God no, once my father rules someone as an outcast, you remain an outcast until the end of days," he sighed and brushed himself off before standing and pacing along his previously trodden path. "Did I do so much wrong in saving the elves, orcs and mages?" he questioned as pained tears laid dormant within his eyes.

"Of course not! Did you not see the way they watched your latest performance, how they called after you? Christ Julian, when you retired to bed, I heard them

whispering about everything you have done for them.
So do not let someone's prejudice ideas of what
should be deemed as perfect, destroy everything
you've worked so hard to maintain." She encouraged
him and placed her hands on his arms to keep him
from turning and pacing again, "I know that Anya
mentioned that a vampires bite is fatal to an elf but
surely if you can get them on your side, then they'll
guide you into the kingdom walls."

"Well my dear, it is funny you should say that," he
chuckled awkwardly and took one of her hands in his
and scratched the back of his neck with his free hand
"I do happen to know of a vampire who is said to lurk
within these woods. But they were a previous
bedfellow...if you catch my drift."

"Oh, did you not part on good terms?" she said with a
schooled expression, and yet the faint pink on her
cheeks betrayed her, as her thoughts ran wild with
images of Julian's lips trailing along her neck.

S. L. Coe

"Rather the opposite, love. But I soon learned –
excuse the pun – hard way that a vampires teeth are
not best suited for kissing a partner below the belt," he
chuckled as he watched the captains eyes widen in
surprise. "Do not worry yourself my dear, I soon
repaid the favour, I never dream of leaving any man or
woman unsatisfied," he winked with a smirk as he
watched her blush deepen.

"That remains to be seen," she smirked back with a
mischievous twinkle in her eye, and by the gods, it was
the bards turn to blush crimson.

"Captain!" he gasped, equal parts impressed and
astonished.

"Bard!" she chimed back and gave his hand a squeeze
of support before she turned to the trees and spoke
"So how do we draw out the vampires, other than by
the obvious methods."

"There isn't a particular way to draw them out, rather we have to break a branch from the oak tree and then call to them, like a siren would call to a sailor" he explained as he lead the captain towards the oak tree that usually sat in the centre of the long enchanted woods. As he stood behind the captain, he snaked his one arm around her waist, and pointed over her shoulder towards the opening in the trees. "Repeat these lyrics after me" he whispered, purposefully keeping his voice low to not draw attention to them before it was time. And yet with his warm breath against her neck, the captain couldn't help but shiver and wrap her fingers around his wrist for some stability. "You do not have to earn my favour. Just, fuck me, you beautiful stranger," he purred the lyrics.

"Julian!" she gasped and pulled her lips between her teeth to keep from making unholy noises around creatures with such sensitive hearing. Her cheeks were hot as she looked up at him, her eyes heavy with wanting.

"Yes love?" he questioned as his gaze flickered from her eyes to her lips and back up before he spoke again, teasing and tempting "Cat got your tongue?"

"Ah- not at all, I just was not expecting you to be so bold," she smirked and met his eyes over her shoulder. She cleared her throat before allowing a seductive hum to leave her lips before she moved forwards, turned to face him and sang "You don't need to earn my favour. Just, fuck me, you handsome stranger." She couldn't help but smirk as she watched his face turn crimson and his hand come to cover his lips as he fought to hold in his whimper.

And yet before the bard could meet the captains eyes again, a dark chuckle came from within the forest. His skin was as black as the night sky, and his eyes a deep blood red. He was dressed head to toe in a deep purple robe, leather boots that reached the top of his knees, a black hooded cloak and little else. "Are we changing the lyrics to suit the suitor now, Julian?" the vampire smiled with an air of playfulness in his voice.

"Of course not, you know the lyrics are best suited to a duet, Nicodemus" he quipped back as he fought off a smile.

"Maybe I do." he jested and offered his hand.

"I can't believe you're still alive!" Julian said as he pushed Nicodemus's hand to the side and pulled him into a quick hug. "I thought you were staked by Apollo."

"Gods no, do you really believe I'd sink as low as to let myself be staked by that rat," he replied with a mock offence and laid his hand on his own chest, just above where his heart used to be.

S. L. Coe

"I'd hope not."

"So why did you lure me out here?" Nicodemus questioned as he sniffed the air at the scent of fresh blood, black veins appeared in his eyes as he turned towards the captain "A human, how quaint."

"No. The Captain is off limits." Julian said with a fierce determination as he moved in front of her and gently held her behind him to keep her as far away as possible from the blood-hungry gaze of the bards ex-bedfellow.

"Ah that's a true shame. I'm awfully starved," he sighed as he flicked his cloak and turned on his heel.

"Wait! I'll strike you a deal," the captain said as she moved out from behind Julian.

"You have my attention," the vampire stated as he leant against a nearby tree with his arms crossed in front of his chest.

'Trust me,' she mouthed to Julian before she turned to the vampire before her and took a confident step in his direction "I will give you 5 ounces of my blood, if you are willing to help us with our quest."

"Which is?" he questioned as he raised an intrigued eyebrow.

"To gain access to the Elven kingdom," The bard sighed -pained - as he met the vampires eyes before looking up to the castle where he used to reside. "I know it is a futile mission, and I will more than likely be turned away at the door but I just want to gain some form of access to the castle, and I can't do that without the two of you."

S. L. Coe

"I'm in."

"That was quick," the Captain spoke as she eyed the vampire curiously and stepped towards Julian.

"Darlin' I want his father punished for what he did to Julian, and if that means fighting off more of my own kind then so be it. If it were not for him, none of us would be walking this plane, and that tavern you stayed at last night, would be in ruins."

"How do you know we stayed at the tavern?"

"You're glowing. It's a glow that only the tavern provides to those of a mythological nature, and with your curse and magic, it is no wonder the tavern swore to protect you."

"I - " the captain blinked as she processed the information and gave a content sigh. "Right, so how do we access the kingdom?"

"First, I require the payment," The Vampire said as he stalked towards the captain and stood behind her. "Julian, do you give me permission?"

"The decision is not mine to make. It is up to the Captain; it is her blood and her body" Julian said as he sat on a fallen log and watched as Nicodemus brushed the captains hair away from her neck and allowed his fangs to lower themselves into place.

"I consent," The Captain nodded as she met Julian's eyes and mouthed ' I will survive'.

'I know you will,' he mouthed back, and audibly gasped as he watched Nicodemus pull his head back before plunging his fangs into the soft flesh off her neck.

The captain gasped and moaned at the sensation as she briefly closed her eyes before focusing on Julian. He looked back at her with such yearning it was hard for her not to reach out to him. He could feel something stir inside his heart. Was it worry, was it jealousy, or was it something far hotter. The bard couldn't tell, but he knew deep down that he wanted to switch places with the vampire. He wanted his lips to be on the captains neck, he wanted to be the one to draw the elicit moans from her – and going by the hungry gaze that the captain had bestowed upon the bard, she wished for that too.

"My, my, I've never known jealousy to radiate itself so powerfully," the vampire teased as he took his teeth out of the Captain's neck and gently pushed her towards Julian who caught her and held her close.

"I don't know what you're on about" the captain
muttered as she clutched one hand onto Julian's cloak
and the other onto her neck.

"Here, drink this," he said as he dug around in his
satchel, handing her one of the five potions that Anya
had purposefully left for them.

"Thank you," she said softly and downed the bottle. A
wave of gold sparks enveloped her and rid her of all
her wounds and ailments that previously lingered
within her body.

"Now, let's get moving. Lest we wished to be caught by
nightfall," Nicodemus said as he sauntered on ahead.

"Are you okay to walk?" Julian asked as he helped the
captain to her feet and took a step forward.

"I believe so," she said as she stepped in time with him "Let us go forth and meet your maker".

"Please never call him that again," he grimaced as he kept his pace in time with the captain and his hands around his lute strap to keep from shaking.

"Would father be better?"

"Perhaps murderer in private. But to his face, only address him as King Nathaniel – unless you want to take a spear to a limb of his choice," Julian warned as he cleared his throat to hide the wobble that threatened to weave itself into his words.

"Did he do that to you?" The Captain asked innocently.

Alas, his silence was answer enough.

Chapter 8: King Nathaniel and the Captains toll.

"I must leave you here," the vampire said with a sigh as he stood at the side entrance to the castle that was covered in thick brambles and dead rose bushes.

"Are you certain you won't join us?" The Captain spoke as she waited for the bard to join them.

"I'm afraid it is not a matter of not wanting too, it is simply due to the fact that I am unable to, for you see the damned king hates the likes of us undead, and so he asked his dutiful mages to lock us out with magic. So unfortunately, my dear, your invite falls on deaf ears," he apologised as he swept into a low bow, placing a gentle kiss on the Captain's hand before standing and making his way over to Julian who stood staring down at a plaque that barely made it out of the grass. "Julian?"

"Mhm?" was all the bard muttered as he crouched and placed his hands over the freshly risen dirt. His mother's grave had been disturbed once again.

"I must take my leave."

"No. Please do not leave me and the captain alone in my father's company, you know what he is capable of," Julian plead with wide eyes as he lost his balance and stared up at Nicodemus.

"My darling, even if I wanted to come with you, I couldn't, you know all too well how tied my hands are." He said as he placed his hands under the bards arms and hauled him to his feet. "Remember, you are no longer under his control. He cannot harm you."

"It is not me I am worried about!" Julian cried as he looked over to the Captain and back to Nicodemus, lowered his voice and spoke through his teeth, "He's disturbed my mother's grave again! He will not allow her to rest, I can feel her torment trembling in the ground. So what's to stop him from doing the same to the captain?"

"That I do not know, but if you must, then use your chaos and allow what is left of your magic to reck fresh hell onto your father. Let him feel your wrath. You have my strength and my word that I will have a ship ready for you by the end of the day after tomorrow."

"But-"

"No buts, you are a bard Julian, and the captain is plenty capable of handling herself should it come to it. So do what a bard scorned does best, and best him with your words. Now I must bid you adieu for the sun is at its apex" Nicodemus spoke quickly as he held a hand up to the sun with a hiss and pulled his hood over his head to protect his thin skin from the harshness of the sun. "Goodbye, good luck, and good riddance, Julian Scott. Captain," he bowed and ran off into the dark depths of the forest.

"Bard, are you okay?" The Captain spoke softly as she approached Julian, who shook like a leaf in the wind as a profound sadness clouded his eyes and he watched as the castle doors and windows began to crack and close in on themselves.

"I'm fine, my captain, you do not have to worry about me," he lied as he met her eyes and pulled his lips between his teeth before taking a deep breath and raising himself to his full height, in order to gather what was left of his bardic performance.

"You don't have to lie to me, I'm here for you," she said as she snaked her hand into his.

"I know, but if I am to break now, I will be made out to be a fool in front of the court and more importantly my father," he said as squeezed her hand and lead them towards the heavy wooden gate.

"Julian are you sure you want to do this?" she questioned as she stopped in front of him, and thus blocked the gate from view.

"I need to speak to the mages and apothecary if we are to find a cure to your curse," he explained as he watched her.

"You a better man than you give yourself credit for," she smiled as she took a bold step forward and wrapped her arms around his waist.

His dangled at his side in confusion as he felt her pull him closer, and with a little hesitation he hugged her back, desperately hoping that she couldn't hear the quick thumping of his heart.

"And your crew are certainly lucky to have you," he smiled back as he enjoyed her embrace. "And it will be a great pleasure to sail under you...with you, it'll be a great pleasure to sail with you," he chuckled as he felt his cheeks flush again.

"I know what you mean, but you best know that I expect you to follow my orders to the T when you sail with me," she smirked teasingly as she broke the embrace and walked ahead of him, cheeks aflame.

"Yes ma'am" he quipped back with a playful smirk of his own as he watched her shiver with anticipation. "But that does remind me, there is a ball tonight, and I am yet to find a partner."

"But I do not know how to dance, other than through drunken frolicking."

"I believe your dance moves at my performance just a few nights ago, suggest otherwise. But fret not, love, I am more than happy to teach you," he purred as he opened the gate and allowed her to enter first.

"Then I will most gladly attend with you" she agreed with a bright smile and mischievous eyes.

"I am pleased to hear it," he grinned back and closed the gate behind him before walking through the grounds of the castle plucking a careful tune to alert the mages and apothecaries of his arrival.

***

"You can't do this!" came the raised voice from just beyond the entrance hall.

"Oh by gods, I can. I am the king of west Draconda and you will do well to remember your place unless you wish for your head to roll on my floor," King Nathaniel spat as he stepped into the equally furious squire who had watched the king throw caution to the wind and exiled half of his court out to the untamed vampires that roamed the surrounding woodlands.

"You may be a king, but you sit on a throne of lies and rule a kingdom governed by nothing but pure unadulterated fear. And I'm sure the son you exiled from the kingdom many years ago would agree with everything that he is," the squire said as she met eyes with Julian over the kings shoulder.

He could swear his blood froze and his heart stopped for eternity as he shook his head and pressed himself against the pillar in an effort to conceal himself from his father's piercing gaze. "Shit. Shit. Shit. Shit." He muttered under his breath as he fought to keep himself from shaking.

"Who are you looking at?" Nathaniel demanded as he looked behind him, his eyes ablaze as they locked onto Julian's lute. "What the hell are you doing in MY kingdom?" he bellowed as he stormed over to the pillar and dragged the bard by the hair until he stood in the centre of the room, shaking like a leaf in the wind. "Speak!"

He fought the urge to curse and spit in his father face, for the captain was only a corridor away and the entire court was watching him. "I was hired as tonight's entertainment," he choked out as he tried to raise himself to his full height and yet, despite how broken he felt, he breathed.

"By whom?"

"I cannot say."

"You can and you will," he said as he raised his heavily ringed fat hand into the air posed to strike.

"I cannot and I shall not, you will never be dignified with the answer. Did you not hear your squires words, or do you plan to kick them out too!" he spat as the last nerve snapped, and he stepped into his father. "You may have once exiled me for freeing those you deem unworthy of life, but the court have spoken and I will claim my place on *that* throne, regardless of your pathetic opinions. For when your heart stop beating, I will dance upon your grave and the world will be right."

"You are an insulant brat! You will hang by the end of the night!"

"Then have me sentenced to the gallows, unless you are too coward to commit to it," he growled and met his father's eyes, his lip curled in disgust.

"Fuck you, you are no son of mine."

"AND YOU ARE NOT MY FATHER!" he shouted and the words tore from his throat and ricochet of the walls, easily rivalling the gasps that came from the surrounding court. His eyes burned with furious tears that he would not allow himself to shed, his whole body shook as he reached for the dagger that the captain had given him only days ago. And yet, as he rose the dagger to strike, his father's hand came crashing down and swiped his face so hard that he fell to the ground. His blood trickled out of the deep laceration that resided high on his cheek. He groaned as he opened his eyes, only to see his father's hand plunging towards his throat.

"Take your hands off of him!" the captain demanded, her sword drawn and moving closer and closer to the king who slammed his son into the harsh marble floor.

"Oh, I think I'll do what I please," he grinned viciously as he chucked Julian to the floor, leaving him limp and reeling from the pain.

"Captain..." Julian cried as he tried to reach out to her, and yet in time to the scrape of metal on flesh, his consciousness was ripped from him and he lost sight of everything around him.

***

"Where is the captain?" was the first demand that left the bards lips as he sprung to sit up from where he laid, and yet he was pushed back down onto the makeshift medic bed.

"Lay down, you'll tear your stitches!" The squire cried as they drove the needle through the bards cheek.

"I'll tear my own stitches out if you don't tell me where she is," he said through gritted teeth, his hand coming to grasp at the stitches to show just how serious he was. But before his piano player fingers could weave their way into the thread the squire slammed the bards hand back onto the bed and pinned it there with magic.

"Julian Scott! What has gotten into you, do not tell me you burn for the captain."

"I...I do not believe I have to answer to you," he muttered as he turned his head away from the squire, tears pricking the backs of his eyes.

"Oh Julian..." the squire sighed as they sat at his bedside and paused their healing, "you know your heart is a fragile thing, I remember the last ballad you wrote about heartbreak, you made me cry for weeks. So please, darling prince, tell me what it is that troubles your heart so."

"Do not call me prince," he snarled in disgust and curled his lip before looking back at the squire. "Ethra, I have not burned for anyone since my mother's death. Or rather murder... and I fear, if I allow myself to love her then she will succumb to the same fate. But at the same time, every thought I have of her makes my heart race and she is the only woman who makes me feel alive. Even on that bastard ship where they tortured us until we bled, she was the one who encouraged me to keep fighting, and if I lose her then... I have lost myself."

"My dear boy, you will not lose her."

"How can you be so certain?" he questioned with a wobble in his voice.

"Because I healed her myself. She is in full health and more than ready to sail Draconda's seas. Although she did shed several tears of those black gloves covered in ivy."

"What happened to them? What day is it?"

"It's Saturday. Your father stole them," they said bluntly and began to finish what they had started.

"Shit!" Julian cursed under his breath and hit the bed below him with his free hand.

"Julian, what is it?"

"Those gloves were what I made for her. They kept the moons affects at bay; they started off her curse for a day at most. And now she will suffer because of me."

"Tell me about this curse, perhaps I and Maria can be of assistance."

"It is not my curse to share, and I do not know much about it."

"Time is off the essence, tell me everything you know," Ethra said as they nodded towards the door where from beyond whispers of the kingdoms guard could be heard.

And tell her, he did.

***

Hours had passed since the squire had attended to his wounds, and his lute was thrown haphazardly on the corner of his bed, and the bard himself laid stiff on his side, shirtless and wallowing in his own misery. The bruise on his cheek had changed from a light purple to a deep violet tinged with angry red streaks and the pounding in his head grew stronger with every minute that passed.

"Bard?" The Captain's voice came softly through the door, but it went unanswered as his skin stung with the agony of healing. "Bard, I do not care if you are naked

S. L. Coe

- I live on a ship with 50 men, if you do not think I have not seen it all before you are severely mistaken. So if you do not answer me, I will make my way in," she warned and pushed the door open further.

"If you are here to convince me to show my face at the ball, then please do not attempt to, I have already decided I am not attending. But if you are after a dress then you will find one in the draw fourth from the bottom," he mumbled as he remained on his side and kept his hand over his father's fingerprints that resided on his neck, a reminder that no matter how far he ran, his father would always know of his location.

The Captain gasped as she saw the scars from the whip littered across his back and the bruises from his father scattered along his arm. "My darling bard, please face me," she said softly and sat on the other side of his bed and gently brushed a strand of hair from his face.

"But I have failed you," he muttered as he leant into the captains touch, a faint heat dusted his cheeks.

"You could never fail me," she promised as he gently pushed his shoulder so that he laid on his back, and yet he would not allow his eyes to meet hers – in fear that he would break beneath her gaze. "If you do not look at me, I will sit on you and then you will have no other choice but to look at me," she said, her voice low and welcomingly dangerous.

"You wouldn't," he half smirked as he gave her a sideways glance.

"You doubt me?" she questioned almost playfully as she kneeled on the bed, ready to move.

"Until you prove me wrong, Captain," he said as he matched her tone and raised an eyebrow, welcoming her next move.

And by the gods did she take the opportunity as she swung her leg over his waist and straddled his hips, her arms situated on the headboard before her. "Now bard, do I have your undivided attention?"

His face flushed crimson as he took a deep breath to calm himself and met the captains eyes, although his own threatened to flick down to her lips. "You always have."

"Good, so now tell me without the barriers, without withholding the truth, what has your mind so scattered," she demanded as her thighs tightened on either side of him to ensure that he could not move, although in doing so she had to force her lips together to keep from making an ungodly noise as she followed his eyes.

"You. You have my mind scattered," he declared as he reached for her hand and placed it over his heart. His bare skin was hot to the touch as his heart thumped against his chest, "Do you feel that, that rhythm is the anxiety you brought me when I thought my father had done something to you."

"I do, but you have to understand when I saw him throw you to the floor my own heart threatened to leap into my throat and onto the floor with you," she said as she took his hand and placed it upon her heart, "Do you feel that? That rhythm is the one you bring me every time you appear. It is the rhythm that I walk too, so please forgive me if I have overstepped a boundary by going after your father – but I will not stand to see you be harmed."

"Nor will I you," he said as his eyes ran over her face as he admired her flushed face.

The Captains chest heaved with every intake of breathe as she met his eyes, her hands travelled from his chest to his cheeks – careful to avoid the growing bruise – she could feel him growing gently beneath her and she fought the urge to moan as her eyes fixated on his lips – mirroring him completely. "Julian..."

"My lady..." he purred as he brushed a gentle hand through her hair and smiled gently as he watched her melt into his touch.

"I bur- oh god!" she cried as her hand slipped off of the headboard and she fell towards the bed. And yet she never met it, as his hands landed on her hips to brake her fall.

"I told you that I would let no harm come to you," he smirked as he tipped his chin towards him and ran his thumb across her lower lip, her tongue flicked the top. "You make resisting you almost impossible," he sighed as he pressed his forehead to hers.

"Who said I wanted you to resist me?" she challenged as she ran her fingers along his jaw and moved forwards until their bodies were pressed flush against each other.

"What about your honour?" He questioned as one of his hands gripped her hip and the other ran up her back and into her thick wavy locks.

"Forget my honour, I am a captain, that I am content with. But it is my heart that longs for you."

"And I you," he whispered as their faces were mere inches apart, their lips almost brushed as they spoke. "I will not let anyone bring harm to you, under any circumstance."

"You have my word; I shall protect you until the end of my days," The Captain whispered as she moved to close the gap, he yearned for her so much it almost physically hurt. And yet just as their lips were about to brush, the bedroom door was thrust open by the squire.

"OH, I'm sorry Julian, I was not aware you and the captain were pre – occupied," the squire said as they put a hand over their eyes.

"I- we were just - " he stammered before a chuckle left his lips and he gave a look of an apology to the captain, who simply shook her head and smiled with a mouthing of the word 'soon enough, bard' before

climbing off of him. "What is it you need Ethra?"

"The ball it begins in half hour, and you are the

entertainment," she said, in a tone that could only

come from a mother who knows how to get her son to

listen.

"But I already said that I am not attending."

"You're going!" both Ethra and the captain spoke at

the same time before erupting into a bundle of laughs.

"Okay, okay, stop my sides hurt." The captain said

through laughter as she looked at the confused look

that had etched itself onto Julian's face. "I will explain

everything in time," she said as she attempted to regain

control. "But first I require a dress."

"And I will be pleased to dress you," the squire said as she opened the draws and began to riffle through each gown. "Julian, if you wouldn't mind."

"Of course not," he said as he took the lute from his bed and his covered suit off of the curtain rail that surrounded the top of his four poster bed. "Captain, Ethra, I shall find you after my performance, we need to discuss your curse and bringing an end to my father," he said and forced himself not to flinch as he recalled the memory of his beating.

"Good luck, and if you should need me then do not hesitate to find me," The Captain said with a curtsy. "I promise you he will not come within a foot of you."

"Be careful" he said and with that he exited from the room and bolted down the hall to the baths where his faithful servants were waiting to bathe, clothe and talk with him.

Chapter 9: Treason trapped on the

performance floor.

"My lord, my lord, my lord! Please calm yourself!"
The servant cried as he watched Julian pace the floor,
his hand trembling as they ran over the marks on his
throat and his brown curls a mess upon his head.

"How, how do you suggest I do that Kyle, if it were not
for me the Captain would not be facing a charge of
treason!" He cried as he began to strip himself of his
upper clothing and head towards the large bath that
resided in the centre of the room.

"A treason charge are you absolutely certain?" he said
as moved to check the bath water and collect the bards
clothes from where they had been carelessly strewn
across the floor.

"Because she went against my father, to protect me."
He explained and asked Kyle to avert his eyes as he
removed the lower half of his clothing before sinking
into the warm bath.

"But that does not mean he would place that charge
upon her, we would know by now" Kyle explained as
he gestured to the rest of the servants who were
preparing Julian's suit for tonight.

"Then you clearly do not know my father" he said as he rested his head on the back of the tub and in doing so allowed for his bruises to become public.

"My lord your neck!"

"Hmm?"

"Who did this to you?"

"I think you know the answer to that question."

"But I thought the beatings had stopped," he said in a hushed whisper and placed a gentle hand on the bards naked shoulder and crouched at the side of the tub.

"They only stopped because I ran," he gulped and gasped for air as his hands shook under the water.

"Would you like me to heal them? I believe I still have the correct salve stored away nearby."

"No. Please leave them be, I want them to stand as a reminder of how vile their precious king is if you do not follow his rule." He stated disgust thick in his voice as he held his hand out for a towel and stood when it was handed to him. "If I am to go into battle, then I want to go into battle fully prepared."

"Of course my lord. However, I must ask if you will allow me to speak freely?"

"I shall."

"How do you want to bring an end to your father?"

"I thought you would never ask," he said as he climbed out of the tub, wrapped the towel loosely around his waist and headed straight for the weapons cabinet that resided just below the window. "I believe we shall use this," he said as he held the hilt of the metallic rose thorn wrapped dagger with great caution.

"My lord, we cannot. You and every elf along his bloodline will die if you do."

"Then it is my life that shall end."

"This is madness, what about your sister at the inn, is she not part elf?" The servant pled as he watched Julian hold the blade up to the light.

"Fuck," he cursed under his breath and slammed the blade down on the counter. "Then how do you suggest we end this nightmare?"

"Fret not, I have a plan."

"Then prepare me for battle."

***

As the night drew on and the patrons began to fold into the ballroom, the bard and the captain were nowhere to be found. Instead they lingered in the corridor, unsure of what to say or how to interact as everything within them burned to touch the other. Julian couldn't help but admire the way the sapphire blue of her gown seemed to shimmer in the candlelight before it gently softened and transformed into a luscious sea foam green. Gold jewels were placed delicately across her neck and the deep V of neckline which connected oh so perfectly to the gold band that resided over the smallest section of her waist. And as she twirled in a circle with a coy smile, the peacock feathers made themselves apparent as they brushed the floor and swept up her legs until they reached the slit on the left side that left her dagger clad leg exposed to the elements.

"Do you like it?" she smirked as she watched his pupils blow wide with lust. Although she was unaware of it, her eyes did the same as she finally placed her glance onto his own doublet that was made out of the finest black silk and held emerald green vines around

the arms, collar and cuffs. And thus it lead to the vocal
point of the outfit – his crown and bruises.

"My lady, you look absolutely ethereal. Are you quite
certain I have not died and gone to heaven?" he
smirked back as he watched her run a nervous hand
through her hair.

"I am quite sure you are in the land of the living," she
quipped back as she drew closer to him "Although it is
quite a shame that you are so well dressed, I miss your
usual bardic dress."

"And I miss your wonderful hat and corset," he sighed
as he met her eyes "But desperate times call for
desperate measures."

"Indeed they do, and so my bard, would it be a crime
to ask you to kiss me again?"

"Love, I'm afraid our lips never touched before," he said as he gently placed his fingers under her chin and tipped her head so that she could meet his eyes.

"Then perhaps it is time that we change that," she suggested as her cheeks grew warm beneath his gaze, her legs pressed together to alleviate the growing pleasure, and yet she struggled to keep her eyes on his.

"Only if you say my name," he smirked as he placed one hand on her waist and cupped her face with the other as he bent down to meet her height.

"Julian...please," she whispered as she stood on her tiptoes.

"It would be my pleasure, Willow," he purred and brought his lips to hers so that they were mere inches away.

Their breathes mingled together as electric sparks seemed to fly between them. Her hands roamed his chest and his stayed firmly planted on her hips as he pulled her closer. And yet, just as their lips were about to brush Anya flew around the corner with a loud crash.

"Fuck," he cursed under his breath as he withdrew from the captains embrace. "Soon, love, soon I shall kiss you."

"Every time," The captain groaned as she pressed her back against the cold wall to alleviate the heat that grew within her. Her heart raced against her chest as she brought her hand to her lips and reminisced on the way their lips almost brushed, and by gods did she yearn for more. She yearned for his hands, his lips, his heart.

S. L. Coe

The bard was silent for a moment as he caught his breath and forced his body to calm itself. "What are you doing here?" he said through gritted teeth "What about the tavern, is it safe? Did something happen?"

"No, no, Julian, do not fret the tavern is safe." His sister explained as she placed a hand on his shoulder, "I have left it in the hands of the orc Hestia twins...did I interrupt something?" she said as she looked between the flushed face pair.

"You could say that" the Captain said under her breathe as her eyes flickered from the bard to Anya. "But pray tell, why are you here? I thought you said you couldn't leave the tavern."

"Normally I wouldn't, however Kyle and the squire sent their finest men to fetch me after they caught wind of the plan."

"The plan?" The captain questioned as she looked between Julian and Anya.

"He plans to kill our father."

"ANYA!" Julian whisper shouted as his eyes narrowed.

"Julian, you cannot keep her in the dark about this. It is life and death, and if what you told me is true, then we cannot leave her out of this."

"Alright, I am officially confused, can someone please explain what is going on?"

"I am planning to end my father's reign," he said as he sunk down onto a wooden bench that was placed precariously against the stone wall. "This," he said as he pointed towards the unhealed marks on his neck

S. L. Coe

"was the last straw, not only for me but for the servants and the reminder of the court who still believe in me and our fallen siblings."

"I'm in," The captain said as she withheld a gasp at the sight of the Bards bruised neck. "Are you still able to perform?" she questioned as she sat beside him, gently moving his collar away from his neck in order to see where the bruises ended. It was just his luck that the deepest part of the bruise resided just on top of his voice box.

He sadly shook his head. "Not unless they are healed, and if I heal them now the plan will fail."

"Then allow us to sing for you, your fingers still work, yes?" she said as she looked over to Anya and waited for a nod of approval, and once it was received, she spoke again "Then you will play the melody and we shall sing the tune. Granted it will not be a show stopping performance but I shall lay my life on the line

to save you."

"I assure you it will not come to that," he said as a

determined fire burned bright within his eyes and he

stood, threw his lute strap over his shoulder and held

his arms out for the Captain and his sister to take a

hold off.

"Into battle."

"To bringing an end to the kings reign."

"To killing my father," they toasted with a nod as the

two ladies hooked their arms around Julian's and the

three of them walked down the corridor and into the

ballroom - servants gathering from either side.

This would be a night to remember, one that would go up in flames.

***

"Take your positions," Julian whispered to his sister and the Captain as they let his arms go and proceeded to find their starting point, but before the captain could be three paces away he reached for her hand and pulled her towards him, he brought her knuckles to his lips and pressed a gentle kiss to them, "I will find you after this."

"I know you will." She whispered back and gave his hand a squeeze.

"Good. Now go." He commanded and allowed her to weave her way through the crowd before he parted the crowd and shrugged off of his doublet as he allowed it to hit the ground with little care. His lute was brought to his front and his crown stood tall upon his head as he reached for a goblet of wine either side of him, in his left he held the poison, in his right he held the antidote.

"Ah, I am so sorry my darling court, I did not mean to arrive so late to my own promised performance, but it appears the king had other plans and thus I am unable to sing tonight," he explained as he bowed to the

crowd and allowed the collar of his shirt to slip down
and expose the painful bruises, "But I do not wish for
this night to be one tainted by bad blood, and so, I will
ask you all to join me in a toast," he said as he passed
the goblet in his left hand to the king, who although
eyeing it suspiciously brought his to his lips. "Cheers!"
he said as he watched the crowd take up a goblet of
untainted wine and swig as he downed his own, and
thus riding his father of any chance he had of curing
himself.

The wine would not take effect until the second dance
had found it's natural end but the confused look on his
father's face was enough to fill the bard with a renewed
sense of confidence as he began to strum his lute and
used his magic to light the freestanding candelabras
that stood on either side of the captain and Anya.
"And so my beautiful audience, whilst I cannot sing
tonight, my sister and my companion most certainly
can, and without further ado I welcome you to open
your ears to my newest composition: So the king(dom)
shall fall," he said with a bow and began to hum the
opening notes so that the two ladies knew when to
begin.

𝄞 "I will not become a victim to your tyrant rule.

You may disturb a grave to gain your pleasures.

But I am not one of your ragdolls who you can
control.

* * *

With your honeyed words and crimson eyes, you
expect.

Everyone to fall at your feet, but you might wish for the
court to know.

Oh Hoh oh!

you might wish for your court to know, just how much
you yearn

to manipulate their power and use it to grow your
army.

My mother was not one to follow the rules.

And so you buried her under the fallen fern.

You sold her jewels and tightened your rules,

But for your son

But for your son

Your beatings are next to none.

And now it is with that tainted wine.

Your life becomes mine.

So enjoy your time and learn from this rhyme,

That the end of your reign is nigh"

By the end of the song the crowd was alive with applause and gasps of horror as their eyes travelled from the bard and his companions, to the king whose anger had manifested itself in hardlines and blood vessels that had popped across his cheeks. His feet pounded on the hard marble bellow and he B-lined straight for Julian. But before the king could get within an even foot of the bard, the court, the city mages, the captain and Anya had surronded Julian. They brandished their swords and readied their magic.

"If you take another step towards our prince, it will not only be his wrath that you face, it will be ours too," Kyle spoke up as he stood at the front and center of the battle. And whilst the bard cringed at the use of his title, his eyes brimmed with grateful tears but he would not allow them to be shed.

"This is treason! All of you are to be sentenced to death!" the king bellowed as his body shook with unrivalled anger. And yet the court erupted into a fit of laughter, which hid their looks of fear.

"I'm awfully sorry my king, but it appears your prison guards are also on our side," Kyle gestured to the guards who stood with their sytches poised and ready to strike, yet waved to the king none of the less.

"So what's next, you banish us from the castle? Hmm?" The Captain piped up as she gestured for the crowd to part to allow the bard to pass through the center.

"Oh no, there shall not be time for that, for I fear the poison is working far quicker than we had anticipated," Julian hissed, his lip curled into a vicsious sneer as he walked up to his grotesque father and king.

"You drank the wine too, how are you not poisoned?" the king spat his question and almost allowed for his fear of death to shine through his false bravado.

"Oh no father, I drank the antidote," he spat and threw his hand around the kings pimple covered neck, his face inches away from his fathers ear as he lowered his voice and with drew the captains dagger from his pocket, plunged it into his fathers side and whispered "Enjoy the land of the dying, for your journey will never end. Perhaps now my mother can enjoy her afterlife in peace." He ripped the dagger from his fathers side and took the coin purse that hung on his father belt, and descend the stairs with a freed smile on his lips. Juliens' shoulders seemed lighter. His confidence came back in leaps and bounds as the crowd watched with eager eyes.

"Please, start the music and enjoy the night, for tonight your freedom is yours. Fret not, about the king, he shall bother you no more. I thank you all for everything you have done for me tonight, it will not go unforgotten. So please, my friends, allow the night to begin," he beamed as he bowed to the crowd who eagerly moved to either the bar or the dance floor.

"You did it!" Anya cried as she threw her arms around her brother and almost knocked him to the floor.

"Ugh, I forget your're part orc sometimes," he chuckled as he caught her and hugged her back, "but yes come the end of the second dance, the deed will be done."

"I am so proud of you," she smiled as she moved him to stand on his feet and allowed him out of her embrace, instead she turned him to face the captain. "Now go get that kiss."

"Anya!"

"Just go," she laughed and made her way over to Kyle and the gaurds.

"Thank you Captain, I could not have done any of this without you," he smiled softly as her as she stood before her him toying with the material of her dress.

"I'm certain that is not true, but I am glad I got to be here with you" she smiled back, "It was truly riverting to see you in such a commanding position"

"Why thank you, did I sell it well?" he said as he lowered his voice so that only she could hear. "Because I was fearing for my life."

"You sold it incredibly well, in fact, I think that performance was worthy of a captain."

"Oh" he said suddenly flustred as he met her eyes, unable to form a coherent sentence after such high praise "You have a lovely voice."

"Really?"

"Indeed, I look forward to hearing more sea shanties when we board your ship" he grinned and raised his hand as the band began to play a low saucy song that would surely raise the tension by a notch or two.

"I'm sure that's not all you'll hear."

"Now you have my undivided attention," he smirked as he lead her to the dance floor.

***

"Now my lady, I cannot promise you that my dancing is as adequete as the music I perform, but I will be sure to give you a show," he promised as he bowed and placed a gentle kiss on her knuckles before standing, and holding both of his hands up in front of him about 5 centimerters apart.

"Do not lie to me good sir, I have seen you perfom countless times, so much so that I know you know how to command a dance floor," she playfully suggested as she held her hands up to his, only a mere inch away.

"Well then, I suppose it is time we put your skills to the test," Julian said as he stepped into her and she stepped back as they began to turn in a circle. "Speaking of, what is life like on the ship?"

"As in my ship?" she said as their hands rose above their heads and connected before coming down into the position of the waltz.

"Hmm, I have never set foot on a ship such as yours, perhaps a small sail boat to get from coast to coast, but never anything as grand as The Black Bess," he explained as he span her out and allowed her to dip before he pulled her back to him.

"You know the name of my ship? I'm impressed," she smiled as they swayed chest to chest, her eyes flickered from his lips to his eyes as the two of them slipped into the next position. "Well, it depends on what role you would like to take, personally I would like you to act as my second in command. But that choice remains yours."

"And what would I do in that position? Would I be made to follow your orders?" he questioned as a sly smirk grew on his lips, and he pressed a gentle kiss onto her neck as the two of them twirled across the dance floor.

"You seem rather fond of that" she purred as they landed against a pillar. Her chest heaved as she gasped for breath.

"Indeed I do," he agreed as his eyes darkned and ran over her body admiring every beautiful, powerful inch of her body before they returned to her lips, "Perhaps, you would order me once again?"

"Just...kiss me, Julian," she sighed in anticipation, her hands clinged to the front of his shirt.

"It would be my honour," he purred as he cupped her face and brushed his lips against hers oh so gently, and by god he wanted so much more as his heart hammered against his chest, he rested his forehead against hers before he spoke again. "I fear I cannot be gentlemanly with you."

"Then do not be," she said as she pressed herself against him and wrapped her arms around his neck "Allow yourself to give in to what you want most."

"I want you."

"I am yours."

And with that their lips crashed together as his hands found her waist and pulled her flush against him. She tugged on his hair earning herself a moan from the bard. Julian couldn't help but press her into the pillar as she ran her tongue along his bottom lip and plead for entrance, which he gladly gave. A shiver ran down her spine as their tongues ran across each other and their lips brushed over and over again until the pair were gasping for breath, and yet neither of them wished to part as the captain brought her leg up from the floor and hooked it around Julian's waist. Julian couldn't help but chuckle seductively as he ran his hand up her thigh and give it a squeeze when he felt her buck against him.

"What's so funny?" she panted as they broke the kiss,

"It's not funny, it's more enderaring," he purred as he tilted her head up and kissed below her jaw "...just how eager you are for me."

"You are a fine one to talk," she smirked as her hands ran down his chest and to the growing bulge in his trousers, "I've often dreamt about this moment," she purred as she gave him a gentle squeeze before bringing her hands back up to where was socially acceptable.

"My lady, if you continue down this path, I fear we might gather more prying eyes," he said as he did his utmost to withhold a moan.

"I do not mind an audience."

"Usually, I would not, but we are in the process of committing high treason," he said as he reluctantly broke their embrace with one final kiss.

"That is true," she nodded and looked at him with lust blown eyes, "Just one more taste and then I promise we can get back on track."

"I believe I can indulge you in that," he purred as he bent down and kissed her cheek with a smirk "The rest will come later, I assure you."

"You are a harsh tease," the captain groaned playfully.

"But that does remind me, I found a mage that knows about the curse" he whispered as his eyes drifted over to his father who was covered in a thick sweat and gripped onto his throne with an iron grip. "I fear we have just under half an hour to find them."

"We will find them in twenty minutes," The Captain said as she took his hand and moved them closer to the bar and thus hiding them from his fathers gaze. "What is their name?"

"Do you remember the squire who healed you, Ethra? Well in my blind state of panic when I awoke after the beatings, she said that she had healed you, and so during the planning of our treason," he explained before taking a swig of wine out of an abandoned goblet. "I did some digging, and it turns out Ethra had suffered the same curse as you only ten years prior, and so I figured if we can find them perhaps they will provide us with an explination or a location we could go to find a cure."

"That is all well and good, but do we not need to find the person who curated the curse first?"

"Do you know who made it?"

The captain hesistated and ordered two more fresh goblets of wine before she answered "not exactly, I know the reason but not the curator."

"And what reason is that?" he enquired as he gestured to an empty table and they sat together.

"It was a long time ago, when I first comandered a ship and stole a crew. Their was a thousand of us on board, and the storm was beyond our control. And at the time, I was not aware of the pirate code, I was just a mere fifteen year old lass who wanted to have a purpose in life, and we set sail against everyones best intrest..." she explained with tears swimming in her eyes as she took a shaky sip of the wine "and we came

up to a particuarly rocky section of sea near Death Isle
that I believed we could manuever through with
relative ease, however that proved to be false as we
soon crashed into the side of the rocky hills that delve
below sea level, and the ship went down. And in the
process my pervious crew lost their lives. I was the only
member of the crew left alive...I thought I would be
left for dead. But it appeared their was a dark mage –
who remained faceless – and said that the only way for
me to repay for my sin and bring back the souls of the
dead, was to take on my moonlit curse."

"Oh Captain; it was not your fault, you did not know,"
Julian spoke softly as he took a sip of wine and placed
a comforting hand on hers.

"I wish that were the case. But if I am to find the cure
that the curator stated is avalible, I do not want."

"And why is that?"

"Because I will have to willingly take the life of a
thousand people," she muttered and brushed a tear
from her cheeks.

"We will find another way," The bard promised as he
met her eyes, "What happens if you reach twelve
moons?"

"Then she will be forced under the surface of Death
Isle, and be made to live out a further twelve moons as
a half dead being," Ethra said as they emerged from
the shadows.

"But surely there is another way to cure this, it doesn't have to come to that does it?"

"It depends on how many moons have already passed."

"Four moons have passed this year," The captain admitted as she toyed with the trimming of her dress, "I am bound for deaths embrace."

"Do not say that, I will find an alternative!" The bard excalimed as he squeezed the captains hand, "I will not allow it."

"Julian is correct, I do know of one other mage who is capable of doing a spell that could provide you with more moons and thus in the process give us more time."

"Who is this mage?"

"Appollo Tome." The squire admitted.

Julian's eyes widened as his entire frame began to shake with fear and deeply buried hatred that he held for the rat. "No, Ethra, you must be telling some sick joke, he will not cure her, he will kill her."

"My lord..."

"No. Listen to me. I delt with him many years ago, he is the reason I was exiled, he took my ears, my heritage and title away from me. Do not allow him near the captain," he demanded as he stood. But in doing so, he regretted every move, as in the doorway stood none

other than the rat faced smarmy bastard. Julian's blood
ran cold and all the air in his lungs was robbed from
him as he slowly turned his head to look at the captain.
A tear slipped from his eyes as he mouthed to the
captain to "Run," but it fell on deaf ears as the captain
was forced to stay in her seat by Apollo's magic.

"Julian..." The captain whispered desperately as she
tried to reach for him and only caught his finger tips.
He tried to grip onto her hand but his were frozen at
his side.

"Oh my my, I do love how you thought you could
escape my power," Apollo smirked darkly as he tilted
his head and gave a jerk of his left wrist, and in doing
so a loud crack ricocheted off the walls, and the bones
in Julian's right hand snapped one by one.

"What do you want from us?" Julian hissed through
the pain and gave a quick blink and you miss it look of
'get to the tavern' to Anya and the rest of the court that
remained on his side, and with the mages mist
sheilding them from site they fled as fast as they could
back to the tavern.

"Oh, I want nothing from you, other than your
popularity. But as for your captain, I want her to fulfill
her promise and then die."

"You can go to hell," Julian spat as he forced his body
to move so that he was standing in front of the captain,
"I will happily send you there myself if you take so
much as a shuffle towards *MY* Captain."

S. L. Coe

"Your feet," the captain whispered as she dropped her key beneathe his boot, "if this goes to hell, use my key and call parlay and you will find me."

"I will not let it come to that," he whispered back as he kept his feet togther and kept the key hidden from sight.

"Then perhaps, I shall take her from you," Apollo grinned wolfishly and curled his fingers so that only his top two and his thumb were showing, and then with a mumble of an ancient witches chant, threw them across the other and thus he rid the captain from sight.

Julian's heart lept to his throat and he saw red as he saw her vanish "What did you do to her?" he growled and lunged forward brandishing a long forgotten sword.

"That's for me to know and for you never to find out," Apollo laughed harshly and repeated the motion before vanishing into nothingness.

"No..." the bard muttered as his breathing became ragged.

He held the key in his hand, his eyes wide and lost as he looked over to where Kyle and Ethra stood next to his dead father, "Tell me theres a way out of this. Tell me that this is just an awful nightmare that I will wake up from!" he cried desperately.

"My lord, I do not know what to tell you" Kyle said as he drew closer and reached out to offer a comforting hand.

But alas, the bard flinched away and held his broken hand to his chest. "Do not touch me. And you!" he hissed, his voice full of venom as he span on his heel and looked Ethra directly in the eye "I told you not to involve yourself with Apollo Tome, and yet you did not listen. And so it is because of you, that my Captain, my only companion in this souless world, is missing. And poetentially dead."

"My lord, I did not know he was this dangerous."

"And yet you trusted him," he spat as he threw his crown across the hall in an attempts to rid himself of any connection he had to royalty.

"Let me make this right, I will do everything in my power to help you find her."

"You will do far more than that." He growled "Get rid of the kings corpse, and do not contact me unless you have information about the captains whereabouts. Am I clear?"

"Crystal."

"Then be gone. Kyle, ready the mages. We will not stop searching until she is found."

"As you wish."

Chapter 10: When the ship is a-rocking...

"I've found her! I know where the Captain is!" Ethra cried as they ran through the corridor, breathless and red faced.

And yet, Julian could not stand the mere sound of their voice let a known the words of false hope they spouted. "Ethra, you lie. You cheat. You beg and steal. You greet death as though he was an old friend, although he quite clearly is not. So do not look me in the face and attempt to fill me with false hope." He spat, his eyes ablaze, and his fists clenched at his side.

"Julian, I am telling you the truth, you have to believe me," she plead as she followed after him. Her pace several feet slower than his.

"Oh, like I believed you about the cure. How, I , foolishly allowed myself to confide in you without thinking twice. God, I am a fool. Stay out of my sight if you know what is good for you. I am headed for the tavern, do not attempt to follow me," Julian hissed as he pushed past Ethra, collected his lute and belongings from where they stood at the castle door and strode headfirst into the open world.

***

His mind was everywhere, all the songs that he had
composed over the course of his healing now seemed
to vanish into thin air as he fretted over the safety of
his muse. But as he started to run in the direction of
the tavern, he could feel several eyes on him, and
despite the sunlight one set of eyes strode forth.

"Nicodemus? What are you doing out here, you'll
catch your death," Julian whispered as he pushed him
back into the shadows of the trees.

"I am coming with you," Nicodemus said with a fierce
determination as he tried to move back into the
sunlight but he was once again stopped by the bards
strong arms.

"You will die!"

"And that is a risk I am willing to take, please allow me
to take it."

"I cannot."

"Julian, my dear friend, I can see the fear in your eyes,
I can smell the anxiety and trepidation in your veins,
and I know from experience that anxiety and
trepidation do not fare well on the battlefield" he
advised as he sat Julian down on a fallen tree, sitting
opposite on a stump.

"But what about the captain? She has been taken by
Apollo Tome, and if he so much as lays a finger on
her, I swear to the high heavens I will find a way to end
his life as I did my fathers!"

"And that I do not doubt, but you cannot go into battle by yourself and expect to come out the other side alive. And yes, you may be a bard and a famous one at that. But that does not mean your fame and bravado will save you. You need to allow yourself to rely on your friends."

"What if Tome comes after your clan, or the members of the tavern? What happens if he manages to convince the Bards guild to come after me again? I could not live with that amount of death on my hands."

"It would not be on your hands. It would be and will be on mine, for I have already spoken to my clan and they are far more than willing to accompany us. I assure you; we will find your captain. Will you now allow me to accompany you?"

"But what about the sunlight?"

"Julian. Stop fretting, I have already covered all basses. Do you have the key that the captain left you?"

"I wouldn't dream of leaving it," he said as pulled the key from underneath his shirt, and dangled it from its makeshift necklace before he tucked it back under his shirt.

"Then let us go." The vampire spoke as he stood and hauled Julian to his feet before he ran ahead through the forest and lead the way to the tavern.

***

The summer air was thick with humidity as they drew closer to Anya's tavern, and yet Julian could not shake the scent of burning, no matter how hard he tried.

A flurry of sparks hit his cheek, and he immediately knew it was Nicodemus.

His eyes widened as he looked towards his immortal companion.

"Nicodemus you're burning!" he cried as looked between the distance of the tavern to where they stood.

"I'm fine, really," the vampire wheezed as smoke began to drift from the hem of his trousers.

"Fine? Fine? You're on fire!" Julian yelled as he threw his cloak over Nicodemus and barrelled him in – headfirst – into the tavern.

Nicodemus bared his fangs and growled as he fought against the bards hard grip, "What the devil are you playing at Bard?"

"I am saving your life, and do not even dream of biting me. I am not above using elven magic to turn you human," he said as he ripped his arm away from the vampires ever growing fangs.

"You wouldn't."

"Do not test me."

A clatter of pots and pan resounded through the almost barren tavern, and through the smoke of the hearth Anya emerged, a thick layer of dust and smoke covered her face and clothes, but she marched onwards to the bard and vampire who sat across from each other, barely making eye contact.

"What the hell are you two playing at?" Anya questioned with the voice of an irritated mother.

"Nicodemus was burning and he refused to go inside, and so I had to tackle him in doors otherwise he would have become a pile of dust."

"Dear Bard, you truly do love to exaggerate!" Nicodemus said as he attempted to stand and yet due to his severe reaction to the sun his legs buckled and he went tumbling towards the table.

"You call this exaggerating! Anya, please, help this fool."

"Bring him around the back" Anya said as she stood on the opposite side of Nicodemus. Together her and Julian hauled him into the far shader backroom that allowed only the smallest amount of natural light to shine through.

"Are you all right? Did the patron's make it back safely? Did Apollo follow you? Did you see the Captain, at all?" Julian fired question after question at Anya as he dug around in the potion cabinets, His mind ran at hundred and forty miles an hour, swirling with dangerous thoughts. His hands shook as he passed the anti-burn serum over to Anya.

"Julian, breathe," she said as she applied pressure to his hands to keep him grounded and distracted, "I am fine, Apollo would not ever dream of touching me. Everyone is safe, I instructed them to go home to their families and recover from the events of last night. And as far as I am aware there is no possible way for Apollo to enter my tavern and live to tell the tale. But as for the Captain, I am unsure. I haven't found anyone who has seen nor heard of her."

"Fuck…" he cursed under his breath and ran his hands through his hair in frustration. "Is there not another pirate we could ask? A ship I could commandeer and hope to run into her out on the open seas?"

"Well it is funny you should say that," Nicodemus piped up as he allowed Anya to work on his wounds "I think, when I visited the shipping quarry over a month or two ago, I found a few lost pirates who were trying to find their way back to a ship called The Black Bess."

"How many moons ago was that?"

"Two I believe, but why does the moon matter?"

"Because, my good man, it was precisely two and a half-moons ago today that the captain and I were kidnapped and placed upon a bandits ship. And she mentioned to me that her ship was called The Black Bess, and so, what if those estranged pirates you found were actually members of her crew who were simply trying to find their way back to the ship!" Julian exclaimed as his eyes twinkled with hope.

"That is not beyond the realms of impossibility," Anya said as she dug around in the potions cabinet in hopes of finding the correct potions to fill a survival kit long enough to last through the seasons. "Go to the shipping quarry, you never know. You may well find her crew and if you find her crew than you can find the Captain."

"But what about the tavern? What about Nicodemus?"

"I shall be fine, and so will the tavern. I promise you that," The vampire promised as he stood from the table and began to lead Julian to the front door.

"Take these with you, it is only small, but it will keep you fed and warm for the unpredictable months to come," Anya smiled as she handed Julian a satchel filled with a bed roll, potions, several bottles of ale and mead, an amulet of health and a map of where a large sum of treasure was rumoured to have been placed. "And do not allow your heart to fret over us, if anything goes array then I shall send a courier to find you. And lastly, dear brother, remember that we love you and do not wish for you to be sentenced for treason, and thus we shall fight tooth and nail for you."

"And I shall do the same for you, now the pair of you stay out of trouble and I shall return as soon as I am able," Julian promised with a bow and gave the pair a

quick hug before he then decided to leave the tavern
and head over to the shipping quarry via horseback.

***

When Julian finally reached the shipping quarry the
night air had turned chilly and the rain clouds were
almost ready to burst as the dock and quarry sprung
into life, full of chatter and bartering amongst pirates,
sailors and the tavern maidens who offered their
services to anyone of quality.

As Julian wandered the dock he checked every name
and signature that resided on the side of several queen
Anne ships, and yet he couldn't shake the feeling of
being watched. With every step he took, the sound of
a far shorter, a far louder footprint seemed to grow
and get closer to the bards back.

It wasn't until Julian was in the process of attempting to
board a ship which he had only read the first section of
the name off, that the short footsteps finally spoke up
in a rough accent, "Oi, bard, you shouldn't be
attempting to board unknown ships."

"Please enlighten me then good sir, where else am I
supposed to find the ship I am after?" Julian said
without sparing him so much as a glance.

"That would depend on which ship it is, and why it is
you are after the said ship" The dwarf said as he strode

forward and stood in front of the Bard as he demanded the attention he rightfully deserved.

"I am after the Black Bess, I am in search of Captain Embers, she was taken from me by a pitiful rat faced man – named Apollo Tome – and I fear.." Julian explained and took a brief pause to settle his anxious breathing before he continued, "I fear that he may have done something to harm her. So unless you know where I can find the Captain and her ship, I beg of you let me be and search in peace."

"And what is the captain to you?"

"That is something we have not yet had the opportunity to discuss, but I burn so deeply for her, I fear it could put the sun to shame, and I believe she feels the same for me."

"But what makes you feel as though you can find her ship?"

"I am sorry sir, but are you apart of her crew, or are you working for Tome?" he said as he span on his heel and leant against the door of the crew quarters.

"Indeed I am, and I do know the whereabouts of the Captain, but how do I know I can trust you?"

"She gave me this key, and told me to say Parlee? Paarl...par..." he stumbled over his words as he pulled his makeshift necklace from his neck and held it up in front of the dwarf.

"Parley is the word," the dwarf explained as he looked at the key and held it up to the starlight before nodding and handing it back to the bard, who quickly placed it back on his neck.

"Then I call Parley, please, I need to know that she is safe. You can even cuff me if you fear that I am a danger to the crew," he plead as he held his wrists out – ready to be cuffed and chained.

"Fine. I shall take you to her. Now tell me bard, what may I call you?"

"I am Julian Scott, heir to the elven throne, and the infamous bard of West Draconda. But I prefer to go by Julian. What may I call you?"

"I am Thorian Storm-Dweller, and whilst you do seem like a trustworthy fellow, I shall cuff you for both yours and the crews protection."

"Thank you Thorian."

"Do not thank me yet," Thorian said as he took the cuffs and chains from his belt that sat high upon his waist, almost hidden by his long ginger beard, and locked them around Julian's wrist and feet before leading him off of the ship and further down the shipping quarry where the sailing ship was awaiting their arrival – more than ready to take them to the Black Bess that was residing close to Mages Corner.

***

As the night sky began to deepen in colour, the water became far choppier as it met the harsh evening summer breeze that was made colder still by the protective force that the Mages often placed around their quarter of Draconda to ensure that it kept unwanted visitors at bay. Julian shivered and hissed as the wind licked at his exposed wounds, and he cursed the fact he allowed for his hands to be bound. His fingers began to freeze at the tips as his lips were turning blue. Elves such as Julian have always had an issue circulating warm blood during harsh cold winds.

"Are we almost there?" Julian questioned as he attempted to clutch at his shirt and curl up in an effort to conserve whatever heat he had left in his body.

"You're in luck, we're just pulling into the docks now," Thorin said as he pointed over the top of Julian's head towards the dockland that was littered with ships of every size, shape and colour. But of course, it was The Black Bess that stood the tallest and beckoned the bard ever closer.

"Wait here, I shall see if the captain is ready to receive you," the dwarf said as he rowed the boat into the dockland and climbed ashore before he strode towards the ship.

And thus, he left Julian stranded in the cold, with both his feet and hands bound to the bottom of the sailing ship.

Minutes seemed to tick by unceremoniously as Julian tugged at the chains in a futile effort to free himself, and as he looked to the boat he noticed that the only windows that were lit by candlelight were that of the captain's quarters and his poor heart soared with joy as he saw a shadow shuffle from where he suspected a four poster bed was to the door. And as his mind began to reminisce on the more pleasant memories they shared at the ball, a small smile spread across his face and for the first time in a while his heart felt warm and complete.

"Captain!" he bellowed from the small sailing ship in hopes that he would hear her voice again, but alas he was met with anything but silence.

"Oi! Bard, are you going to come aboard or are you just going to sit out in the rain like a wally?" Thorin called as he strode back towards the dockland, his axe swinging behind him with every step.

"Well I would love to come aboard, although it seems I am in quite a predicament...you left me tied to the ship during a storm," Julian groaned as he tugged on the chains again. "Care to unchain me?"

"If I must," Thorin half joked as he bent down to unchain the bard and looked back towards the ship, "You're a lucky man Julian, I know many men upon the ship would love to earn the captains favour."

"Indeed and I shall do my best to keep in her favour. Is she well? I trust she is not harmed?" he questioned as he leapt from the boat and headed towards The Black Bess with sore wrists.

"As far as I can tell, and from what I have been fortunate enough to hear, she appears to be the same as she was when she was taken from the ship several months ago," Thorin said as he ran to keep up with the bard, for the three foot and two inches difference in their height meant that Thorin had to take six extra paces to keep up with just one of Julian's.

When Julian first boarded the ship, he didn't know where to look for the mast stood at twenty four feet tall and spanned the distance of a hundred and three feet. The ship's exterior was made from Draconda's finest cherry - red oak, and the ropes were tied and bound with a thin sliver of gold embroidery to keep them from fraying. "Hello, fellow travellers, it is a pleasure to sail with you," Julian rambled as he walked towards the Captain's quarters, more than ready to swing open the doors and embrace the captain.

But his plan was foiled as two large fae gentleman stood on either side of the door and placed their spears across to prevent the bard from going any further. "The Captain is not ready to entertain," the elder fae spoke.

"But I have already called Parley, she is expecting me," he explained as he took the key from around his neck and attempted to duck beneath the spears.

"She is not decent-"

"I beg your pardon?" Julian said as he raised a scrutinizing brow at the two fae. It wasn't until he heard a soft breathy sigh did he realise what they meant. His face grew hot as he listened again, and heard his name slip from her lips. "Ahem, gentleman if you would please stand aside, I need to speak to her – directly and in private."

"What is your name bard?"

"Julian, Julian Scott," he repeated as they began to part for him and allowed him and only him to access the door.

"Take good care of our Captain" they said with a bow and blocked the view of the door from the remainder of the crew.

"Oh, I intend to."

***

As Julian sauntered into the room, the air seemed to grow hotter by the second. He couldn't help but smirk as he leaned against the doorway and watched as the Captain ran her hands along her exposed chest and drifted them lower as she bit her lip.

"My gods..." Julian whispered under his breath as he slowly placed his lute down on the floor, his trousers were already feeling tight against him as he walked towards the desk where the Captain sat with her legs wide open, exposing everything to him.

"Julian!" she cried out in ecstasy; her eyes barely fluttered open as she felt a wave of pleasure wash over her.

"I'm right here, love," he purred as he ran his fingers along the inside of her wrist, barely ghosting her skin. Her eyes snapped open as she looked at him, her eyes were still glazed over with lust but her smile shinned brighter than the stars.

"You found me!" she cried as she stood and jumped into his arms and almost barrelled the two of them over. His arms tightened around her waist as he pulled her flush against him.

"I promised you; I would never stop searching. And if I knew the show would be so delightful, I would have found you sooner," he smirked as he gently brushed a stray strand of hair from her face and allowed his thumb to brush against her cheek as his eyes flickered from her eyes to her lips.

"And I shall explain it all later, but right now I want...oh," she smirked as she felt his bulge twitch against her thigh. Her hands ran up his chest and down his arms until she found his wrists.

He was weak to her touch, and by gods did he yearn for more as her hands pinned his arms above his head and she began to pepper kisses along his neck.

"My lady..." he moaned softly as he gently rolled his hips against hers in an effort to gain some friction.

"Use my name," she demanded as she gently bit down on his collar bone and suckled until she found his sweet spot and left a dark mark. She couldn't help but clench her thighs together as his whimpers and moans went straight to her core.

"Willow, let me kiss you," he begged as he nudged her legs apart and pressed his knee against her already soaked core, which earned him a rather wanton moan.

Her lips crashed onto his as her hands cupped his face and she wrapped her leg around his waist, desperately rutting against his already tented trousers. His lips were hard against hers as he poured every ounce of love and adoration he had for her into their heated kiss, his hands couldn't help but roam the soft skin of her thigh. A dark chuckle slipped from his lips as his fingers ran in the shape of a figure eight over her soaked sex. "Oh my love, you are truly soaked," he purred into her ear "And the fun has barely begun." And with that he swept her off her feet and wrapped both of her legs around his hips as he sauntered over to her bed. His wet shirt clung to his muscles and wet her front as he gently placed her down onto the bed, his gaze was deliciously lustful as his eyes roamed her exposed body.

She reached for his hand but Julian simply pushed it aside with a playful Tutt "Ah, ah, ah, my love. Tonight is about you."

"But I want to touch you," she whined as she met his eyes, and he cursed himself for being so weak for her already.

"And you shall have me, soon," he purred and laid beside her as he ran his hand along her body he played special attention to the sensitive skin at the top her thigh, never quite going where she oh so desperately wanted him.

His lips followed his hands as he moved to kneel between her knees and pulled her towards him by her knees.

Julian couldn't help but smirk as he watched her arch her back and grind against thin air, as plea after plea left her lips. "Use your words love."

"Please!"

"Please what?" he questioned as he placed her left leg over his shoulder and moved her knickers to the side, his lips mere inches away from her dripping pussy.

"Please touch me! Eat me out, anything Julian! Please, I need you!" she cried as her hands curled into the soft silk blankets beneath her.

"Oh your wish is my command," he grinned before he ran his tongue along her slit and began to move it in a figure 8 route. One hand flew to his hair and pulled it gently, begging for more. "Careful love, if you do that I might not be able to last the night" he laughed darkly, the vibrations just made her pulse more.

"Oh I will make sure you will," she cried as she bucked against him.

And with that his tongue and lips found her clit as he allowed his first two fingers to gently work their way into her. As he curled his fingers, she clenched around him already running on a high from her ruined orgasm. He couldn't help but savour the taste as his tongue lapped at her wetness, his spare hand ran down his chest and between his legs as he began to palm himself in time to the rock of her hips.

She couldn't help but writhe against him as she felt the warmth grow in the pit of her stomach and she knew that it wouldn't be long before she was falling over that delicious edge. And with that Julian sped up his fingers and made sure to hit the point that made her see stars every time, his own moans rumbled low in his throat and boarded on a growl as he could feel his own climax coming.

His cock twitched in his hand, and he decided then in that moment to give her his undivided attention as he held both of her legs open on his shoulder and began to move his tongue in a way that he knew would have her coming undone in seconds.

Her hands reached for anything in sight as she pressed her lips into the mattress to avoid making so much noise.

But alas Julian raised his head from between her legs, his lips and chin glistened with her slick, he smiled as he cooed "No my love, do not hide your noise. I want your crew to know how well I fuck you."

"Fuck! Fuck! Fuck!" The Captain whimpered as he dove back down and did everything in his power to make her cum, and fuck did she. Her hips spasmed against his face until she was practically riding it, her hands clung to the thin fabric as she called out his name and came undone and laid back against the bed breathless and mostly spent.

"Kiss me," she grinned, practically glowing as she beckoned him down to her, and he was well and truly willing to oblige as he laid between her legs and placed gentle kiss after gentle kiss on her lips. Her nose scrunched a little as she tasted herself, but she moaned none of the less as she felt him grow even harder against her core.

The kiss grew far more heated as she found her energy again and hooked her leg around his hips before flipping them so that she was on top and he was trapped beneath her, well and truly at her mercy.

She smirked down at him as she watched his eyes widen and grow darker with lust as she stripped herself of her remaining clothing, until the only barrier that sat between the two of them was his cotton trousers that now left very little to the imagination.

"Do not hold back from me, bard," she purred as she ground her hips agonisingly slow on his clothed

erection, a breathy sigh left her lips as his hands flew to
her hips as he attempted to guide her movements.

"Gods, I need you," he said as he bucked up into her
and whimpered at the feeling of her hot sex that was
already leaving a wet mark on his trousers that he so
desperately wanted to rid himself of. His face flushed
red as he felt her warm hands drift to the waist band of
his trousers and pull them down with such efficacy that
left him gasping with need.

"Hmm," she pretended to pause for thought as she
climbed off of him and sauntered towards the dresser
purposefully swaying her hips as she went. As she dug
through her dresser she purposefully spread her bare
legs and made sure that he got a good show of the
mess he had made of her. It was with a devilish smirk
that she turned around and dangled a pair of elven
cuffs from the top of her finger. Julian's heart
thrummed against his chest as his cock stood to
attention and ached for her wrist around him.

Their gaze sent sparks flying through the room as she
straddled his hips and took his hand in hers. "May I?"
she questioned as she raised a playful eyebrow and
moved so that the tip of his erection lingered at her
eager hole.

"Fuck yes," he cursed under his breath and held his
wrists out for her crossed, and more than ready to be
restrained by her and only her. His breath caught in
his throat as he felt the cold metal come in contact with
his soft skin, several curses tumbled from his lips as

her breasts hung in front of his face. And it was with a mischievous twinkle in his eye, did he get the idea to capture her nipple in between his tongue and teeth. As he gently tugged and swirled his tongue around her sensitive bud, her moans grew in volume and her shaking hands could barely focus on closing the cuffs.

"Julian...if you continue..." she murmured as she pressed her forehead to his before beginning to trail kisses along his chest and neck, leaving small purple marks as she went.

"I know," he said with a mischievous grin and bucked up to meet her hips and ran his cock along her slick folds.

"Shut up," she laughed softly as she captured his lips in a searing kiss that left the pair rutting against each other like an animal in heat until she reached behind her and lined him up with her entrance.

"Make me," He dared her as his eyes lingered on hers and a cheeky grin danced on his lips.

With a deep breath and another tender kiss she sunk down onto his erect cock and took him all the way in. Julian couldn't help but watch – breathless and flushed – as the captain rolled her hips slowly at first and encouraged him to move in rhythm to her. And after a few unsuccessful out of time ruts, the pair found a steady rhythm that left the Captain bouncing on his cock and the bard beneath her trying to keep his moans to himself.

Her nails ran down his chest and followed the outline
of his muscles as she admired the way they pulsed and
twitched beneath her touch. "You are ethereal," she
whispered softly as the muscles of her thigh began to
burn and she settled for rolling her hips rather than
bouncing.

"And you are a goddess," he replied as he started to
take over the lead and began to thrust deeply into her,
a deep growl left his lips as she pinned his hips to the
mattress.

"Ah, ah, Bard. I am in control now, you made me
wait. Now it is your turn to use your words."

His breathing turned rugged as he fought to keep his
hips still despite his growing hunger. "I want...I need
you to fuck me. I want you to make me cum," he
begged as he arched his back and tugged on his chains
as he yearned to touch her.

"My, my, the bard begs well," she teased as she leaned
forwards and entwined her hands with his and began to
rock against him. Her lips lingered mere inches away
from his as she tilted her head and allowed for her
tongue to trace the outline of his lips. "Come undone
for me, Julian," she purred and sped up her thrusts
until her high was fast approaching.

"You first, my lady," he growled as he thrust into her, a
thin sheet of sweat covered the pair of them as the
sound of skin on skin filled the room. His skin was on
fire as she allowed her hands to roam wherever he

would allow them to go, and he was dangerously close to the edge, and yet; he did not want the night to end. He gasped as he felt her clench around her, her legs were starting to shake as he continued to roll his hips and rut into her.

Their tongues danced against each other as she held his hands tighter and allowed herself to fall over the edge. With a shout of his name she came hard all over his cock. Her juices ran down his still hard cock and he placed several gentle kisses onto her cheeks and lips as he whispered sweet nothings to her.

"My love, you have not finished," she whispered as she steadily began to roll her hips again, bringing herself to the brink of overstimulation as he tried to thrust into her and keep his orgasm at bay.

"I cannot finish inside you," he whispered, "us Elves...have particularly potent...cum."

And she knew what he meant, even if he wasn't explicitly obvious. "Then I shall make you finish elsewhere," she purred as she climbed off of him and instead took him in her hands and began to stroke him.

He couldn't help but watch with dark and lustful eyes as her pink tongue flicked against the tip of his dick and ran along his slit before she engulfed his still hard cock and began to bob her head in a steady rhythm that soon had him bucking and aching for more.

His hands rattled against the chains as he fought to unlock them and bury his hands in her hair.

And within seconds he had managed to gather enough magic to unlock the cuffs and his hands found their way into her thick curly locks.

With a nod of her head, she allowed him to push her head down, as she bopped her head, he thrust into her mouth and shuddered against the mattress as the knot in his stomach unravelled and he came down her throat. She pulled up for air and immediately he beckoned her to him and pulled her into a deep kiss that set her skin on fire all over again.

"I burn so deeply for you Captain Willow Embers," he whispered as he pressed his forehead to hers, a grateful smile on his lips.

Her eyes shinned with satisfied tears and her skin seemed to glow with bliss as she cupped his cheek "And I burn deeply for you too, world famous bard and King, Julian Scott."

"That was amazing," he chuckled as the two of them flopped down onto the queen sized mattress.

"You were amazing. Hell Julian if I knew you had that skill, I would have pulled you aside at the ball."

"And miss the anticipation?" he teased with a playful wink.

"Round two?" she smirked as she looked up at him hopefully.

"Let me catch my breath, and then I am all yours for the next five rounds," he grinned as he pressed a soft kiss to her temple and pulled her into a long warm embrace.

"You best hope I can walk tomorrow; I still have a crew to command."

"I make no promises, Captain."

Chapter 11: A morning of bliss, stolen once again by mentions of Jome.

"Oh rusty hook of the deckhand below, keep careful eye on my captains soul..." Julian hummed as he stummed his lute as quietly as he could to keep the captain from waking.

"What are you singing, bard?" The captain mumbled as the soft sunlight danced through the window and she softly stirred in its' warmth.

"Back to calling me bard, are we Captain?" he playfully teased as he put his lute aside and raised his arm to allow her to lie on his chest, and she gladly snuggled down onto his chest and listened intently to the quickened pace of his heart.

"Back to calling me Captain, are we?" she chuckled and ran her fingertips in gentle patterns over Julian's naked chest.

"Touché."

"But I'm curious, what were you singing?"

"I was attempting to compose a song worthy of you. I wish to perform for you at the next tavern we run into, but I am unsure if I should keep the song in English or switch to Elvish," he explained as he gently ran his hands through her hair and pressed a soft kiss to her temple.

"Could you not mix the two?" she questioned as she lifted her head to look at him before turning to her front and looking at him, yearning for a kiss.

"I could, but I fear I would face a charge of treason...again...or loose followers and as a bard, which is not something I wish to risk," he said and gently cupped the Captain's face and rubbed his thumb along the top of her cheeks before pulling her into a warm lingering kiss that made butterflies flutter in their bellies and the sun grow brighter with every second that lingered. Her hands rested over his as she pressed herself against him. She couldn't help but smile into the kiss as his hands roamed from her cheeks to her waist and he held her in a comforting embrace.

"Do we have to leave this room?" Julian asked between kisses.

"I fear my crew will be stirring soon," she sighed as they parted.

"What is it you would have me do today?" he asked again as he kept her close to him and admired the way the sun danced around her eyes.

"That is a very good question Julian-"

"I like when you say my name," he whispered as he stole another kiss from her lips and prevented her from fretting any further.

"Hmm, if you do that again, I will never get to the list," she laughed but relented and relaxed as she kissed him back and ran her hands down his chest, "If you let me tell you about the list, I promise to reward you in kind."

"My love, you do not have to do that."

"Nonsense, I want to. I like sharing myself with you, and after last night I am more than ready to share more than just my body with you."

"And I you. You already know, my heart belongs to you," he promised as his brilliant ocean blue eyes sparkled in the sun.

"As does mine yours. But in front of the crew, I fear we must put up a front."

"I understand," was all that he muttered, but his heart did not falter, for Julian was all too familiar with putting up a front to serve a greater society – including entire courts and taverns - to keep everyone happy and out of harm's way.

"As for the rules, I only have a few," she began, and sat up in bed so that she could keep his focus strictly on her. "First, every crew member from deck swabber to first mate must be in bed by 8pm to ensure that everyone gets sufficient rest. Second, any treasure found must be shared equally amongst the crew. Third, if anyone is caught stealing from another crew mate, they will be marooned without food and water on any distant island, never to be rescued. In the same breath if they are caught lying to any member of the crew, then they too shall be marooned."

"But what about us?" he whispered.

"We are different. It is not a lie; it is a safety measure." She reassured him and gave his hand a squeeze before she began to list the remainder of her rules. "Four, no child under the age of ten may sail upon my ship – it is not safe, and we do not have enough food to keep it alive. Five, we must come ashore every five days, be that to regather energy or to check in with other crew members I do not care. We must find shore. And lastly, every twelve moons, every member of the crew must leave the ship without me."

"Am I included in that final rule, for we only have nine and a half-moons before it comes into play."

"I...no, Julian...you shall be exempt from that rule, but please do not fear me when you see what the twelfth moon causes."

"My darling Willow, I would never dream of doing such a thing. You saw me when I was at my worst, allow me to do the same for you."

"It shall be done," she said with a gentle smile and pressed a kiss to his cheek, "Thank you for listening to me."

"You need not thank me; I would listen to you speak for hours if you would allow me to."

"You would be the first," she muttered as she reached for the hairbrush that resided on the floor next to the bed. "Could you braid my hair?" she questioned almost sheepishly.

His eyebrows knitted together as he only just heard her mutter. "Does your crew not respect you enough to listen to what you have to say?" he questioned as he ran his fingers through her hair before brushing it out until it was smooth enough to braid.

"They do for the most part, but when ale and mead is involved then their willingness to listen to me, soon goes out of the window," she sighed and lowered her head so that Julian could braid her hair from the nape of her neck to the ends of her hair.

He could barely contain a groan of frustration at the thought of his captain being disrespected by the very crew that sailed underneath her, but it was with a great restraint that he allowed himself to remain quiet and focus on the Captains curly waves.

"There are a few members that have staged a mutiny against me, but thankfully Thorian, Alicia, Jones and Juliet were there to overrule and keep the mutiny from happening."

"I would like to meet them, and Thorian again. He seemed quite a nice fellow even though I feared he would have my head with that brilliant axe of his," the bard said as he finished braiding the Captain's hair and looped either braid so that it stood as a crown on the top of her head.

"He means well," she smiled as she felt the braids, "Why do you think I sent him to find you?"

"That was something I wandered...how did you escape Tome?" he questioned and tried to keep the fear from his voice, but it was futile as his shaking hands and watering eyes betrayed him.

Her heart broke for him, and without a moment of hesitation she leapt forward and enveloped him in the tightest hug that she could muster and pressed her lips against his cheek and then his shoulder as she buried her head in the crook of his neck. "Julian, my love, please do not fret. I am unharmed but my curse has worsened. But I believe I am out of harm's way until that twelfth moon rises." She explained as she felt him shake and wrap his arms around her, almost too scared to let go.

"My dear, I was terrified. I...I thought that he had maimed you, I thought that he killed you. For weeks I didn't sleep, I couldn't eat, if it weren't for my elven blood sustaining me I would have died. But please Captain, tell me, in truth, what he did to you? What is it he has planned for you in nine moons time?" he questioned as he fought for breath and hid his face in her shoulder to keep her from seeing the tears that lingered in his eyes.

"I cannot speak it..." she sighed and rubbed small circles into his back as her heart caught in her throat, "And that is not because I do not wish to tell you. He has sworn me to secrecy and if I so much as imply

what he has done to me, then it is your death sentence
I shall be signing."

"Then sign it."

"I cannot!"

"You can! I wish to save you, and if I do not know
what he has done, then I cannot bring you to safety,"
he cried as he pulled back to look her in the eye,
desperate to show her his sincerity.

"And I believe you! But Julian, I cannot have your
blood on my hands...I have already seen what will
happen, and it is not pleasant. Please, please, do not
ask me to relive it," she begged as several cold tears
slipped down her cheeks.

"I will not, but I do not want to lose you at the hands
of him," his voice cracked as he spoke, cold tears
pricked his eyes as he held her hands in his and
allowed his magic to flow between them.

"Julian..." she whispered as her magic met his, and the
pair shared a bond that no other creature in the
entirety of Draconda would be able to break nor tame.

"I cannot lose you, my love," he whispered and
pressed a kiss to her forehead "And I shall not allow
you to lose me either."

"Then...I guess, we shall die together..."

"Perhaps we shall, perhaps I will hunt down Tome and
find a way to bring an end to his rule. I promise you

Captain Willow Embers, that you shall have your freedom."

"And I promise you, that I will ensure your legacy survives regardless of what happens to us."

"Then it is sealed," he nodded and opened his arms for her embrace, and she dived right into them. And everything felt like she was coming home, she was finally safe.

Finally out of the clutches of Tome's poisonous embrace.

"I'm so sorry," she whispered as she clung to him.

But the bard simply shook his head and brushed a stray curl from her face, "You have nothing to apologise for my dear, I shall keep you safe for the rest of my days." He promised and bent to press a kiss to her lips.

And he knew in that moment, the Captain's heart was his, and his was hers.

Chapter 12: The Bard's performance is fit

for a stage, a ship not so much.

When the two of them finally emerged from the
Captain's quarters she walked with a limp, and the
Bard's neck held far sweeter purple bruises than the
ones that sat just below the surface.

The rain had cleared but the sea beneath them
remained choppy as the crew climbed down from their
previously assigned stations and stood before the
Captain ready to receive orders, and Julian joined
them.

"It's a pleasure to meet you again Thorian," Julian
whispered as he stood next to the dwarf.

"The pleasure is mine; it is an honour to have a bard
upon the ship again. And a good one at that," he said
with an impressed nod.

"You know of my work?"

"Of course, essentially anyone who lives in West
Draconda knows of ya. Have you been living under a
rock?"

"Well, not exactly...but who was the bard before me?"

"He was awful, he couldn't carry a tune let a known
stum a lute. He used to be a rogue thief; god knows
how he made it onto the crew."

S. L. Coe

"Well if it is any constellation to you, I am none of those things and I only have the captains best interest at heart."

"I know you do, now hush up before we get in trouble. You do not want to see the Captain mad."

"Oh I trust her anger far more than anyone's here," The bard said as he took the knee and encouraged the remainder of the crew to do the same. If he were to sail under the captain, then he would do his utmost to ensure she received the respect that she truly deserved. "What are the orders for today, Captain?"

"Arse-lick." Came the comment from a rather scruffy woman who stood at the back of the rabble unwilling to take the knee.

Julian smirked as he bit back a playful comeback that he knew would make the captain laugh but would land the pair in trouble. He met the Captain's eyes and she met his mischievous smirk with a knowing wink before schooling her expression and narrowing her focus in on the scruffy women.

The captains voice lowered by several octaves as she looked to the women, with fire in her eyes and her tricorn hat balanced perfectly upon her head, she bellowed "Something the matter, scoundrel? Do you dare to share your complaint with the ship?"

"No Captain..." the scruffy woman muttered as she lowered her head and kept it down in fear of being scorned again.

"That is what I thought, but please, should you object to my newest crew member then please speak your mind, I'm sure we would love to hear your thoughts. Unless you wish to be marooned."

"You shan't hear another word from me Captain Embers."

"Good. I should hope not. As for the rest of us, we shall be training the bard. I expect you to treat him as one of us, and if any harm should come to him, it will be your head on the line. Savvy?"

"Savvy!" the crew cheered and most smiled as they stood from their position and went over to their designated stations and began to untie the ship from the harbour so that they could set sail.

"Did you want me to have a word with that she-devil?" Julian questioned as he stood next to the captain and fixed his red tunic to better fit the part of the Captain's first mate.

"As amusing as it would be to see her embarrassed, we should wait until we are ashore. I shall deal with her later," the captain explained before she gestured to the mast and ravens nest, "Come, I shall teach you how to climb."

"And my lute, what would you have me do with it?" he questioned as he went to strum it but was interrupted by the captains hand. His mouth popped open with surprise as she took it from him. "Whaa – what are you doing with my lute, love?"

"I am going to place it in my quarters, until your training is complete," she said as she turned on her heel and walked over to her quarters.

"But how can I be a bard without my lute?" he persisted as he followed after her.

"It is not permanent; you will have it back once the training is complete. And besides with a voice like yours, you do not need your lute."

"I feel very naked..." he muttered as he stood on the barrier of her quarters and watched as she gently placed the lute down on his side of the bed.

"Well I happen to like you naked," she winked and blew him a kiss before exiting the room.

"Captain!" he cried, red faced and hot beneath his collar.

"Bard!" she chuckled as she mimicked his tone and re-lead the way over to the bottom of the mast.

***

"How on earth am I meant to reach the top of that without falling?" Julian said as he ran his eyes from the bottom of the mast to the very top of the ravens nest that blew in the wind.

"By climbing and holding on incredibly tight when the wind blows," Thorian piped up as he began his ascent up the mast. "Come on Bard, follow me".

"Catch me if I fall?" he asked the captain before he gingerly placed his hands on the rope and began to climb.

"You'll be fine!" The Captain cheered him on and watched as the dwarf and the bard worked together to climb the mast.

As Julian climbed up the mast, the wind grew in strength and whistled through his soft clothing before it pushed the rope out and pulled it back in. "Curse the gods!" Julian said through gritted teeth who fought to keep his balance.

"Only ten metres to go and then we'll be at the nest," Thorian encouraged him, and held out a hand for him "Come on I'll give you a boost".

"Won't you fall though?"

"Good sir, I've been sailing this ship for the past twenty years, I think I know my way around the ropes. Now do as you're told."

And do as he was told, he did. Despite his shaky legs and trembling hands he made it into the crow's nest.

But alas his training wasn't over yet.

***

Next came the cannons, and those were far harder to manage as through lifting each cannon ball and loading it into the cannon, Julian was covered head to toe in gun power. The hammocks that hung from the top of the ship seemed to swing widely with every wave that crashed into the side of the ship, and Julian was rapidly losing his balance.

"Are ye alright down there, bard?" Thorian questioned as he climbed down the ladder and joined Julian.

"If you count being covered in gunpowder and almost failing to keep ones lunch down doing alright, then I guess I am," Julian replied as he shoved his now grey sleeves of his undershirt up so they sat just above his elbows and went to lift another cannon ball.

"My gods lad, you're absolutely filthy."

"Thanks Thorian," he laughed as he heaved the ball up and into the cannon, ensuring that the cannon itself was full of gunpowder. "But I suppose I would have been cleaner if a certain someone was actually doing their job instead of sitting on a barrel and drinking every last ounce of rum they can find." He said as he glared over at scoundrel who was lounging on the barrel, with her legs up in the air and several empty bottles of rum at her side.

"Ignore her, she's a raging drunk most of the time, I'm certain the Captain will have a few words to say to her," Thorian said as he instructed Julian on how to properly load the cannon without running the risk of setting himself alight.

"That she may be, but it doesn't mean that she cannot pull her weight," he grumbled and followed Thorian's training.

"Just wait until we come ashore and find ourselves in the next tavern, she will become so much worse."

"Then I fear it will be the end of my days."

"The captain would have our heads before she let you do that."

"That is true, she is truly a wonderful woman. I cannot wait to see her in action." He beamed as he looked up to the opening of the trapped door in hopes of catching a glimpse of her, but she was far too busy checking the map in the captains quarters.

"I am not a hic-drunk," Scoundrel finally piped up as she chucked another empty bottle to the floor and stumbled over to where the two gentleman were working.

"Those fifteen bottles say otherwise, love," Julian said as he loaded the last cannonball into the final cannon.

"If you don't like it, then perhaps you would like a drink yourself," she said as she sauntered closer to him, a look of strange lust in her eyes.

"I am sorry my dear but my heart is taken by another," he said as he danced out of her way and towards the ladder, and yet as he went his eyes caught the trail of scales going along her neck and the side of her face. "Are you a siren?"

"I have absolutely no idea what you are talking about," she said with a false determination to exclude herself from the conversation.

"Is he right, Scoundrel?" Thorian said as he too climbed the ladder and gazed upon the scales.

"Please do not tell the captain! I am bound to land, I have been forbidden to enter the sea again," she said as she hastily moved her brassy straw like hair to hide her scales, "she will have me marooned."

"I am unsure of what to do," Julian said as he looked to Thorian, who simply looked back up with a look that screamed 'we cannot leave the captain in the dark about this'. "I am a bard and an elf; your songs will not work on me. So do not attempt it. But as for the others, I do not know if I can trust you around them, and whilst I have only sailed with you for a day, I do not like the way you slack off and tear down those who support the captain. And so, I shall give you exactly one evening to prove yourself to me, before I tell the Captain everything I know. Am I clear?"

"Yes, Mr. Scott," she said and held her head down as she wandered back over to her barrel where she proceeded to clear up the empty rum bottles.

"Then we are understood." Julian said as he climbed up the ladder and onto the deck above with Thorian in tow.

"We have to tell her," Thorian said as he pulled Julian towards the captains quarters.

"I gave her my word, if she does not redeem herself by the time in which we get into a tavern tonight at mages corner, then I shall tell the captain everything," he promised as he lingered in front of the captains doors.

"I shall be right behind you," he said with a bow and turned on his heel, "I'll make sure that Juliette and John are ready for you – it's the sails next!"

"Let's hope the waves die down before that begins," he shouted back before knocking on the Captain's door.

***

"Ah Captain!" he smiled as he watched her mark out the route, "Are we off to anywhere interesting?"

"My bard" she smiled sweetly as she looked up at him and beckoned him closer, "We are off to Death Isle."

"Death Isle? But is that not the place your curse originated from?"

"It is, and I believe the person responsible for creating such a curse, may also be there."

"Is Tome involved?" he said as he narrowed his eyes at the thought of that vile man.

"My love, you know I cannot say," she sighed as she turned to look at him and gently caressed his cheek. He couldn't help but lean into her touch and press a gentle kiss to her palm.

"Then, love, tell me what I can do to help," he said as he wrapped one arm around her waist and held her face lovingly with the other before bending down to press a soft kiss to her lips.

She was like putty in his hands as she placed her quill down on the map and wrapped her arms around his neck before standing on her tiptoes to return the kiss. "Just be yourself and do not question my orders, even if they are strange," she muttered between kisses.

"I wouldn't dream of doing such a thing," he purred and pulled her in closer by the small of her waist and poured everything he had into the kiss.

"The route..." she muttered, although her heart wasn't fully in her words as she ran her hands through his hair and happily played with the curls she found there.

"I suppose, I should be a good first mate and allow my captain to work on the map," he chuckled and gave her a loving smile before he broke their embrace and returned their attention to the map in front of them.

"Would you like to lead the route with me?"

"Captain, I am honoured. But I can barely load a cannon let a known man a ship."

"It is simple, I shall teach you."

"But what if I do not have sea legs?"

"Julian..."

"Okay Willow, you win this one. But in return I would like – if it is okay with you – a book upon sirens and a night in the nearest tavern."

"A night in the tavern I can understand, and I shall grant you with this evening as I am looking forward to your performance and latest ballad...but it is the book on sirens that confuses me."

"Well, you see...I am struggling to tell the difference between a mermaid and a siren – they come from the same family tree – but I need to know how they are similar or even different if I am to compose a song about them and protect our crew from them. For I am safe being both a bard and an elf, but the other men and women upon our ship...they are not so safe," Julian explained as he carefully chose his words and looked at the captain with as much sincerity as he could muster for his half-truth.

"Is there something I should be worried about?"

"I do not have enough information to know that myself, but I promise you by tonight I shall provide you with an answer."

"Alright, I shall find several books for you. In the meantime, please send Scoundrel in here."

"Yes Captain," he said with a bow and pressed a kiss upon her knuckles before he left, grateful that she could not see his face, for his eyes swam with guilt.

"Scoundrel! The captain wishes to speak with you," he cried out as he exited the room and headed to the sails.

"What does she want?" The siren said as she walked nervously towards the captains quarters.

"I do not know, and I cannot say," Julian said as he avoided her eyes and kept his focus on his training. "Goodluck."

Chapter 13: A night in a tavern turned into a

brawl at the bar.

When the morning finally rolled around Julian was sat
on the beach with his trousers rolled up to the tops of
his knees, his feet in the sea and his shirt discarded on
a tree several feet away. The others had decided to use
their extra hour of daylight to stay in bed, but Julian
was determined to not only finish his ballad but also
find out why a siren would be bound to the land. But
alas as he stared out into the open sea and felt the wind
blow through his soft brown locks, his heart yearned to
tell the captain the truth. He had always hated telling
lies, but now that he had lied to the captain, he
couldn't help but keep looking over his shoulder,
expecting his guilt to manifest and follow him around.

"Julian! Oi bard!" Scoundrel called as she ran down
the beach towards him and grabbed his shirt along the
way, "The Captain is searching for you, we're due to
leave port in the next fifteen minutes. I was told to
fetch you, lest I want my head to be on the deck of her
ship. She's a bloody scary women when she wants to
be."

"That I do not doubt," he said as he stood and took
his shirt from the siren before pulling it on in haste to
avoid her seeing the mark placed upon him by the
bards guild many years ago, nor the scars on his back

that had yet to heal. "But I thought that we were not leaving until tomorrow."

"I thought that too, but after I had a discussion with her last night, it appears her plans 'ave changed," she said with a mere shrug of her shoulders and moved towards the seas edge.

"What did you discuss with my- the captain?" he questioned as he picked up his lute from where it laid in the sand and shook out any sand that the wind had blown inside the wonderful instrument.

"There wasn't much in the way of words," she admitted as she recoiled from the seas unwanted touch, "She simply asked me if I was a siren, and if I were, what the hell was I doing on her ship."

"Pray tell, what did you tell her?"

"I simply told 'er that I am not a siren, I just enjoy singing and sometimes when the sea is raging my voice holds a great power."

"Oh gods, please tell me she has more wit then sense, I highly doubt she would believe your words."

"Then you would be right bard, she did not believe me. But she has given me a night at the tavern to prove to her that I am not a siren. And that is why, before ya ask it of me, that we are heading to Death Isle."

"Because sirens are forbidden to enter?" he questioned thoroughly confused.

"No ya daft sod because it is a test of loyalty. And if she finds that I am lying then I shall be left to the ravens and the dragons that roam the skies above death isle. A true punishment."

"Then I will come clean to the captain."

"You can't!"

"I can and I will, I shall find a cure for this 'curse' that you claim to have and that evening in the tavern, I shall bear all to the Captain," he said as he slung his lute over his back and marched with urgency towards the ship, wilfully ignoring the pleas of the siren.

"Julian!"

"No Scoundrel, my mind is made up," he said as he waved her away with a dismissive flick of his wrist.

"Then do not blame me when you feel my talons slash your chest," she muttered as she barged past him and ran ahead – wailing into the abyss of trees.

"Oh Bollocks to you," he cursed under his breath and continued on his journey to the ship. He knew that the siren would find her way back one way or another.

***

When he finally stumbled into the tavern with his lute on his back and his navy tunic neatly tucked into his black trousers, the tavern was alive with the sound of drunken sailors and cheery maidens who danced on tables and sung out of tune to most if not all of the bards song category. He couldn't help but smile softly to himself as he heard the familiar words that he sang at his father's assassination, especially when they came from none other than his darling captain. For she stood on the central table, loud, proud and giddy with a large tankard of ale – her red and black skirt swirled around her ankles as she twirled on the table and grinned as she laid eyes on her lover.

"Julian!" she cried as she jumped of the table and placed her tankard down on the bar as she headed over to him, a loving smile spread across her cheeks, "Where have you been?"

"I was on the ship waiting for you," he said as he tilted his head and gave her a cheeky smirk, "My love, are you drunk?"

"Me? Drunk? No...I am just delaying the inevitable," she laughed although the drink induced red of her cheeks suggested otherwise.

"You know we do not have to travel to Death Isle yet if you do not desire it," he said as he brushed a long stray strand of hair from her face and tucked it behind her ear.

"I wish that were true, but I fear time is running short."

"Then we shall find a way to lengthen it," he said as he raised his hand to the barkeep and motioned for two more pints of mead. "Join me for a dance?"

"I thought you hated dancing?"

"I hate formal forced dancing, performative bard dancing, I love. And dancing with you, nothing could beat it," he smiled and bowed before he placed a kiss onto her knuckles, "So would you do me the honours?"

"Of course, my bard," she blushed, took his hand and guided him towards the centre of the floor and up towards the longest table. The tavern sprung into life again as the resident band begun to strum a joyful tune that only the crew of The Black Bess knew, and the crew banged their tankards on the tables in time before they joined in with the chorus.

"I never knew you were one for tavern games," he said as the two of them span in circles and skipped every time the song missed a beat.

"There's still a lot about me that you don't know yet, and a lot that I wish to know about you."

"And that we shall do, together. I am sure we have many years ahead of us to know each other both inside and out," he purred as he pressed a kiss to the Captains cheek.

"Julian..."

"Willow..."

"Hmm, you make it hard to remember that the crew cannot know about us."

"Perhaps they should."

"But what if they turn against me and start another mutiny?" she sighed as he twirled her into his chest and kept his arms wrapped around her.

"Then they will have me, Thorian, Juliette, John and a heap of other crew members to go through first. Hell, I will maroon anyone who defiles your honour."

"You make a very good argument Julian Scott," she chuckled and tilted her head up to his, her lips just inches away from his. The sound of lute strings and drums got louder and more hopeful as their intense gaze went on. And it was with a swell of confidence that Julian bent down to meet her lips, he couldn't help but smile into the kiss as she felt her relax into his embrace and pull him closer.

"I could not burn brighter for you if I tried," he said softly as they parted for air.

"I fear if I burned any brighter I would put the sun to shame."

"Touché, Captain, touché," he grinned, but before he could say another word she caught his lips in a gentle kiss, desperate to feel as much of him as she could. His laugh rumbled against their lips as he swirled them until the pairs feet tangled and they toppled off of the table.

"Steady on! Get a room!" came the playful chiding of the crew who looked at the pair with a proud gaze and encouraged the bard and his captain to sit with them.

"I shall retrieve our mead and then I will join you," The bard said as he helped the captain to her feet and with a chaste kiss he danced his way to the bar.

The bar was quiet as Julian picked up the tankards, more than ready to take it back to the crew and prepare for his set, and yet before he could even move so much as a muscle – the siren stood before him. Her true image sitting just below the surface.

"You're not going to tell the captain about me, are you?" Scoundrel questioned, her voice full of a lingering venom and her eyes steadily turning black.

"Indeed I am, I'm sorry Scoundrel, but you pose more than just a threat to the crew and everyone you meet. You are a danger to everyone who meets you."

"But you understand that I will be marooned on Death Isle, that is a fate worse than death!"

"No, a fate worse than death would be dealing with Tome and trying and failing to figure out what he knows, and what I do not." He glared as he took the tankards and turned his back to her, "so do not expect me to fall for you failed attempt at friendship."

But it was with those words he signed his death warrant as she screeched into the sky and lunged towards him, with her talons exposed and dripping with venom, she lashed out and slashed his back. His breath caught in his throat as he turned to look at her, and yet he felt the world around him sway beneath his feet. His words died on his tongue, and his breath failed him as he tried to call to the Captain for help.

"Capt...ain" he cried as he stumbled towards the table.

"Bard!" Thorian bellowed as he gestured to the crew to stand and ran to the bards side.

"Julian? Julian, I'm here," The Captain said as she rushed to his side, fully sober, and caught him as he lost his balance, "What happened?"

"Scoundrel happened..." he whimpered as he attempted to use what remained of his elven magic to heal his gaping wound, but it did little to numb the pain.

"What do you mean scoundrel happened?" she questioned as she ran her hand down his back, in an attempt to bring him comfort. But when she reached his lower back, her hand was met with a thick puddle of black blood. "What did she do?" she asked through gritted teeth.

"Captain, she is a siren" Thorian said as he urged the bard to rest his voice, lest he see the day that he can no longer sing. "She knew that our bard would expose her in a song, and so it appears she decided to infect him with a curse that will lead him to lose his mind and rob him of his voice."

The Bard and His Captain book 1: Damn Those Gods
Inkpot

"Is there a cure?" the Captain said as she watched a thin sheen of sweat appear on the bards forehead as he gripped onto the material of the captains skirt in a veiled effort to keep himself grounded.

"Only if you have a copper dagger."

"Does it have to be a well-crafted dagger?"

"No. it need only be a sharp shard of copper and a handle forged of anything, combined and then to dip in the victim's blood, and then she must be slain with it. And our bard will be free, and back to his usual self. But we must act with haste."

"Then RUN to the ship and look in my undergarments draw; I have an arrowhead of copper there and a handle for a dagger in the left side of the bedside draw. Find them and bring them to me. I want to end her. GO. NOW. THORAIN," The captain ordered as she prepared her magic ready to heal Julian. But as Thorian ran at the speed of light, Julian's hand came on top of the Captain's arms and he shook his head.

"But it will heal you."

"It will kill me faster," he choked out as he tried to keep the blood from slipping out of his mouth. "Do not waste...your magic...on me."

"I cannot live without you. I did not wish to sign your death warrant."

"You did not," he said as he snuggled into her lap and tried to keep his eyes open and his agonised scream inside. "I made a promise, I would see you free from harm and free from Tome. I intend to fulfil that promise."

"Gods! Why must life be so unjust!" she cried as she held him as close as she could and gently stroked his hair. "I will make you whole again, I swear to you from this point on, no harm shall come to you."

"I do not doubt you," he gasped, "Do you think he will be long?"

"I hope he will not be." She said as she turned her attention to the door, eagerly awaiting the dwarfs return, "Did you see where that villain ran to?"

"I did not" he sighed as he fought against the urge to close his eyes, "May I sleep until he returns?"

"NO. Julian, you must keep yourself awake. Do not fall into any slumber..."

Chapter 14: A race to save the bards life.

"Is he here yet?" Julian whispered as he stared up at the Captain and admired the way that despite her rising anxiety she was able to keep him calm and safe.

"Not yet, but if he does not arrive soon then I shall search for him," she said softly and brushed his hair from his face.

"There will be no need for that Cap' in," Thorian panted as he stood at the door with the bronze dagger in hand and sweat dripping off his forehead. "How is he?"

"He is surviving," Julian laughed bitterly as he moved his hand to his side and sighed when it came back bloody, "Or just about."

"Come on, up you get man," the dwarf said as he stood at Julian's side and went to lift him before the Captain stopped him.

"What are you doing, if we move him, he will die!"

"And if we leave him here, he will get infected and die painfully. We need to get him to safety, and a healer as soon as possible. Let me deal with our bard."

"Promise me if anything happens to him, you will send word to me immediately," she said as she took the dagger from Thorian and dipped it into Julian's blood before sheathing it.

"I will. Now hunt her down and ensure that her death is seen too."

"Wait!" Julian said as the dwarf had managed to pull him halfway to standing, "Let me steal one more kiss from you, in case it is my last."

"My bard do not talk like that. This is just the first of many kisses to come, that much I promise you," she said as she swept into a low crouch and cradled his face in her hands, pressing her lips onto his and pouring every ounce of love she could into the kiss. His heart swelled three sizes as he found the strength to kiss her back. His hands found her hair and the electricity between them sparked a new life. By gods did he yearn for more as he wrapped his weak arms around her waist and pulled her in close to her as she gripped onto his thin tunic and allowed her lips to linger on his. As he tilted his head, his tongue ran along her lower lip and she gladly allowed him entrance as their tongues danced against each other. She could barely contain herself as they broke apart for air. "I love you, Julian Scott."

"And I love you, Captain Willow Embers," he grinned, full of bliss before he stole another kiss and for once the light in his eyes returned.

"Be brave my love, I shall find you again."

"And I will be waiting for you."

"Come love-lark, let's get you to a healer."

***

The captains lips ached and her throat was on fire as she stalked the border of mages corner, the blood soaked copper dagger held tightly in hand as she went. If she had been born something other than human, her eyes would have glowed in fury. The captain was never one for cruel torture, but this time, this time she wanted Scoundrel to drown in the sweetness of death. Her gaze was narrowed and cold as she spotted the siren in the crowd, and she knew in that moment, it was game on. She would have the sirens head.

"Scoundrel!" The captain shouted above the rabble; her voice stopped the siren in her tracks.

"Captain...you have to understand-"

"I do not have to understand anything. You answer to me, and I shall not have you forget that," she growled, tears of frustration shined in her eyes as she held the dagger out in front of her and backed the siren into the nearest corner. "Now, if you wish to keep that tongue in your pitiful gob, you will answer me. Honestly."

"Please have mercy," Scoundrel said as she held her hands up in front of her face.

"I have no patience for your games," The captain spat, her voice full of venom as she stepped into the siren and stood tall. "Why did you attack the bard?"

S. L. Coe

"He was going to tell everyone what I am! I would die on sight!"

"And perhaps he had good reason, but that does not explain why you decided to rob him of his life."

"I didn't know that else to do, it was me or him and I chose myself. He is an elf, they are filthy—"

"Do not speak such vile rubbish. They are just as human as we are," she said as she shook her head and shoved her hand against the sirens throat and squeezed just enough to steal the air from her throat.

"Captain – I can't...breathe!" the siren choked out as she fought against the captains hand, but alas it was futile as the world around her became fuzzy.

"Oh that is what I was hoping for, now stick out your tongue," she smiled viciously as she reached for a silver dagger that she held between her shirt and corset.

"Why – why- why do you need my tongue?"

"Because liars and traitors do not get to speak."

"Please, don't do this! " she cried. As soon as 'this' left her lips, her mouth filled with blood and her tongue dropped to the floor.

"Like I said, lairs and traitors do not get to speak," she spat as she released the sirens throat, sheathed her silver dagger, pinned the sirens arms behind her back and forced her to walk back to the ship, covered in her own blood.

As the ship came into view, Julian stumbled out onto the deck, covered in sweat but supported by Thorian and Juliette. "Is...is that the captain?" he questioned as he squinted into the distance.

"By gods it is! Is she bleeding?"

"I don't think so Julie, but someone's with 'er. It can't be!"

"What is it? I cannot see from this far away," Julian said as the three of them moved towards the edge of the ship.

"It is the siren, crew make way!" Juliette shouted and gestured for the crew to stand to attention, and by the gods did they.

"You!" Julian hissed as the captain shoved the siren onto the ship and watched as she fell to the floor.

"She cannot speak," The Captain said as she joined the bards side and met his eyes, "Are you safe, did the healer help?"

"My dear, I will be fine." He reassured her, although he was struggling to see, "Tell me why the villain cannot speak."

"I cut out her tongue. But I have left the honours for you," she said as she held the dagger out for him.

"You are quite terrifying at times, love," he said as he raised his eyebrows and gave a half amused chuckle, before curling his hand around hers – and effectively the dagger before he spoke again. "I would rather we do it together, lest we wish to spill more blood."

"On your count."

"Three, two...one!"

And with that the dagger was plunged into the sirens heart, and whilst she could not scream or make a sound, the fear and betrayal in her eyes spoke a thousand words and Julian's breath caught in his throat.

The taste of metal faded, and the skin on his back knitted itself back together. He was finally whole again, and yet the exhaustion was rapidly becoming too much and soon the wood beneath his feet seemed to sway until it was nothing more than a brown blur that was coming ever closer to his face.

"Do we still need to go to Death Isle?" he asked, his voice barely a whisper as he tried to stabilize himself, and yet he found himself in the arms of the captain.

"Indeed we do, but you are out of harm's way now," she said as she softly kissed his temple.

"Does that mean I can rest now? I can barely fight the nights embrace," he sighed and closed his eyes.

The captain looked over to Juliette and mouthed to her 'will he survive the night, if he rests now?', and

The Bard and His Captain book 1: Damn Those Gods
Inkpot

Juliette – in the process of tying the siren up – mouthed back a simple yes. And with that the captain gently roused the bard from his rest and guided him to her quarters.

"Come my love, we shall get you back to health."

"Thank you, Willow," he smiled softly and wrapped his arm around her shoulders, gladly following her lead.

"You are welcome, Julian. I promised you that I would see no harm to you, and unfortunately I have failed you an-"

"Willow, I may be delirious with exhaustion, but you could never fail me. This bout of illness was not your fault. It was that of the sirens, and now that she is dead. I am free, I just need to rest and tomorrow I promise you that we will focus on finding Tome and the cure."

"But..."

"No buts, love. You have nothing to apologise for, and I do not wish for you to drown yourself in guilt."

"Can I make you a new promise?"

"I am all ears," he said as he gently pushed the door to their bedroom open and stepped aside for her to enter first.

"Let me love you forever, and all I ask in return is for you to do the same for me."

"I would expect nothing less," he said softly as he bent his head and placed a soft kiss onto her lips. "Now let us rest, for tomorrow is a new adventure all together."

Chapter 15: The morning letters, a welcome calm before the storm.

"Letters! Come get your letters!" The courier cried as he rang the bell and wandered the docks, dishing out letter pile after letter pile to every ship before he sat himself on a barrel and waited for the responding letters.

"Do you reckon we'll have any from Anya or Nicodemus?" The captain questioned as she sifted through the pile and handed each letter to the corresponding crew member.

"I certainly hope so, I was hoping to return there before everything happened, but alas, plans change. And if she can write to us then I am assuming the best" he admitted as he went through his own letter pile, desperately searching for handwriting that resembled Anya's or Nicodemus' at the very least. "Ah, here we are!" He smiled as he lifted the letter to the sky and admired the way Anya would always use sun magic to make the letters dance and swirl in the sunlight.

"It's beautiful," the captain said as she wrapped her arm around Julian's side and rested her head on his shoulder.

"You know, she never fails to amaze me. Even when we were kids she still made sure that every day had something magical in it, besides ourselves of course," he said as he held the captain close in one arm and used his spare hand to look for Nicodemus's' letter.

"That doesn't surprise me at all, she's always seemed incredibly powerful and enchanting to me."

"She must have got it from our mother."

"Tell me about her?"

"My mother?" he questioned with a curiously raised eyebrow.

"Indeed, you always smile brighter when you think of her, and I like to think that a mothers fondness is eternal," she agreed and encouraged him to sit on the side of the boat with her, and he did, although gingerly for he feared he might just fall in the sea again.

"I do not know where to begin, my mother was absolutely beautiful, she always spoke of wisdom and intrigue, and she would always ensure that we were using our magic for good. When I first told her I wanted to be a bard, I was terrified that she would say – like my father – that it is just a wasted profession, but alas, she agreed with me that it is something that I would thrive in, and she is the one who gave me my lute," he explained as a smile danced through his voice.

"What was her name?"

"Marigold Scott – she refused to take my father's name and quite frankly I am glad she did."

"She sounds wonderful, I wish I could have met her. I will be sure to send her flowers the next time we find ourselves upon the shores of the elven kingdom."

"She would like that. Did you receive any letters today?"

"Only two, but that is not unusual for me. I do not have many living relatives nor friends outside of the ship," she sighed as she looked down at the envelopes, one came from a distant friend who resided on Death Isle, the other from an old flame turned friend from almost a decade ago. "But what did Anya say?" she questioned in a brief attempt to change the subject.

"She said:

Dear Julian, I just wanted to tell you that the tavern is safe, since you left there has been no sighting of Tome although Nicodemus believes that he may be dwelling in one of the taverns just off of the coast of Death Isle, so be careful – we do not want to hear reports of either yours or the captains death.

Nicodemus has made a swift recovery since his attempt to burn to ashes, he's currently taking up residence in one of the spare rooms, I told him that he was free to go but he insisted on waiting until you return. Pay us a visit soon, won't you?

Congratulations on finding the captain, I bet the reunion was beautiful if not extremely eventful. Anyway, I must go tavern dwellers to feed and all, but give my love to the captain and crew. Visit me soon, all my love, Anya." Julian's eyes shimmered with tears of relief as he tucked his letter into the inside pocket of his doublet. He smiled to himself as he revelled in the fact that at the end of the day, everything would be okay and it would work out in the end.

"The taverns safe?!" The Captain grinned as she looked up at him with bright eyes.

"It is! At long last, we no longer have to worry about Tome trying to find the tavern!" he beamed and leant back against the ship.

"I'm so happy I could kiss you!" she chuckled as she surged forwards and almost lost her balance as her legs lifted towards the sky, but he caught her just in time.

"Are you already trying to relive our history?" he teased as he swung his leg over the ship and secured her in his arms before jumping down of the ledge and onto the deck of the ship itself.

"Julian! I can walk by myself you know," she laughed as she playfully squirmed in his arms but that only made him hold her closer.

"Maybe you can, but I quite like holding you like this, perhaps I should carry you to our bedroom?"

"You can't carry me over the threshold, not until we married at least!"

"Oh, so you're thinking about marrying me then?" he teased playfully, although surprise lingered in his voice as he wandered over to the threshold but did not carry her over it.

"I believe it would be nice, perhaps after a year of sailing and adventure, I would be honoured to marry you."

"And I you, it would make me the happiest man on the continent," he smiled softly as he bent down and pressed a soft kiss to the captains lips before putting her back down.

"Onto our next voyage?"

"Most certainly Captain, I will follow your lead."

"Then we best prepare the crew."

Chapter 16: Tonight we fall and become one.

Death Isle was not the stuff of legend. It was not the
terrifying land that Julian had spent hours upon hours
researching late at night, and whilst – yes – there was
old drag marks from where corpses had been dragged
through the street, and heads on spikes that had
decayed so much that they could barely be considered
a heat, it was not anything like he had expected. For
the streets came to life with cheers, groans, moans and
shouts from all walks of life as people traded on the
market and used whatever they had on their persons as
a bartering tool. The streets were well lit, and the
people – who were mostly alive – seemed to be rather
nice and genuine.

And yet despite the crews excitement at the sight of the
many taverns and brothels that lingered along Death
Isle's coastline, Julian sat at the side of the ship, staring
but unseeing as he focused in on the looming cathedral
that looked over the city – but alas, it was not the
cathedral that scared him to the core, it was in fact
what lied beneath. For beneath the cathedral lays the
exact same chamber that Julian had been tortured in
and lost everything he had including the tips of his
ears, by none other than Apollo Tome. And yet before
his thoughts could cause his emotions to spiral any
further, that Captain nudged his shoulder and spoke
softly to him, "My love, are you quite alright?"

"I...I will be fine," he said as he took a deep breath and shook his head to clear his thoughts "I was just thinking about something I would rather not remember nor discuss."

"Was this...was this where you lost your ears?" she questioned; her voice so low that only he could hear.

And yet he could not bring himself to say the words, and instead he settled for a simple nod and looked away to shield his pain from the captain.

"We do not have to discuss it now, nor ever if you do not wish to. But should that day come where you need to say what is on your mind, you know that I am never far away."

"I know," he said, his voice scarcely a whisper as he tore his eyes away from the cathedral and instead focused on the captain. "So my dear, what is on the agenda?"

"Well tonight is meant to be a night of celebration for the locals here on Death Isle, so I suppose it would be rude of us not to join in with the festivities later on this evening. But as for this afternoon, I need to meet with a circle of mages who know the curator of my curse."

"Might I join you in that meeting?"

"You may, although some of the things that you hear, may not be pleasant."

"My dear, I have killed my own father, the idea of pleasant conversation has long since passed."

"Then we best make a booking at the tavern and find those mages."

"Can we aim for a room with a four poster bed with curtains?"

"And why is that?" she asked with a sparkle of mischief in her eyes.

"Let's just say, I wish to spend the night doing whatever my lady asks of me," he winked and shot her a sly smirk before entwining his fingers with hers.

"And what if I cannot wait until tonight?" she said as she fought to keep the blush from rising up her cheeks.

"Then I will tease you until you beg me to take you to our room."

"You're a cruel man Julian Scott."

"And you are quite the temptress Miss Willow Embers," he smirked seductively before bending down to place a loving kiss on her soft lips. She smiled into it and pulled him closer, well and truly intoxicated by him.

***

"Wait!" Julian whispered as he gripped the captains wrist and pulled her towards him, "What if Ethra is waiting in there?"

"Ethra? Why on earth would she be there?" she questioned as a glimmer of fear made its home in her eyes.

"I, I do not know. But before I left the castle, she said that she knew your location and that she knew something about you or the curse, I cannot remember exactly, and I do not trust her as far as I can throw her, especially after she practically fed you to the wolf."

"Julian, if she is in there, then we are lost," she said as her hand slipped from his wrist to his hand, "Promise me, we will not find her in there."

"I cannot promise you that, I do not know where she is now," he sighed as he met the captains eyes and gave her a look full of sincerity "But Willow, listen to me. I am now the supposed king of the elven kingdom, so let me enter first. If she is in there, then she is bound to follow my rule or face a sentence of treason. And thus, I will ensure we have the upper hand, so take the back door and I shall enter through the front. I will knock three times to tell you we are safe, yes?"

"Promise me you will not get yourself killed doing this!"

"My dear, I shall be fine. I have the dagger you gave me several moons ago – pun not intended – I will be safe, and if not then I have lived a wonderful life, especially with you by my side. I will find that cure," he promised and headed for the door.

"Wait!" she cried as she ran towards him and embraced him so hard that he stumbled backwards and knocked into the door.

The once dark house, now burst to life as a harsh orange light filled each room and the door began to move behind him. "Get behind me!" he hissed through his teeth and pushed her behind him just in time for the door to open.

"Who are you?" the prophetess declared as she held a lantern in one hand and the staff of thunder in the other.

"Hello there, my lady, I am here on purely official business," he said as he stretched and stood to his full height, he hated playing the role of royal – be that prince or king – but for the captain, he would do anything "I am looking for two things, firstly I would like to enquire about the whereabouts of my healer and mage Ethra Jailston, and secondly, if they are not present I would quite like to discuss the matters of the moon."

"Ethra is not welcome here. She is not one of us, and she never will be. Should she come here with that pathetic rat faced man in tow then they shall both be sentence to death" she said, the hint of a villainous smile shinned through her words, and in a strange way it delighted Julian – for he knew that his allies now lingered in every part of West Draconda. "As for the moon, I was expecting a Captain."

"I am here," The Captain said as she moved to the side of Julian and bowed out of respect, "I am sorry it has taken us so long to find you, it appears Tome had other plans"

"He kidnapped her from under my gaze, and I could do nothing to prevent it," Julian muttered, and whilst he tried to hide the pain that the memory caused – the wobble in his voice betrayed him.

"Then come in, we shall not be caught or maimed by that man again, that much I assure you. As for a cure, that is another discussion entirely."

"Then please enlighten us, we have all afternoon," the captain spoke as she followed the prophetess and lead Julian inside the house.

"Where do we begin?"

***

By the time the elderly woman – whose greying brown hair that resembled a birds nest – came down the stairs for the third time with a giant stack of grimoires in hand. The clock struck the 14th hour of the day. And Julian was struggling to stay awake as he read passage after passage that said the same thing, and it wasn't until the captain nudged his side did he realize that he had started to nod off.

"I'm sorry prophetess, it must be the left over side effects from the siren's scratch that has me falling asleep at your dining table," he said as he did his best to hide a yawn.

"Do not apologise, the effects of a sirens scratch are never pleasant, believe me, I've had my fair few altercations with those vicious creatures," she said as she rolled up the sleeve of her dress to show him a deep grey scar that wrapped itself around her forearm.

"How long did the effects linger for?"

"Roughly four moons, but there is a positive for a gentleman such as yourself," she said and raised a playful eyebrow that left the captain red-faced.

"Pray tell good lady."

"The sirens scratch truly improves a gentleman's stamina and with you being of elven blood, it heightens the potential for repopulation."

"The first part sounds...delightful," Julian said as he cleared his throat and looked anywhere bar the captain in fear of his body betraying him.

"But you do not like the idea of the second part?"

"Not that I wish to sully your opinion of me, nor do I particularly wish to discuss the subject of my sex life...but us Elf's have a reputation for reproducing incredibly easily."

"I wouldn't be particularly adverse to that" the Captain whispered as she held his hand beneath the table, "if I could bear a child that is."

"Captain!" he whisper shouted in surprise and yet he couldn't help the bright smile that danced on his lips, "we must talk about our future before our evening commences."

"And we shall, but I fear the prophetess might not wish to be a part of that conversation," she whispered back as her bright smile mirrored his before she cleared her throat and focused her attention back to the task at hand. "So prophetess, tell me, how are we to find a cure before that 12th moon rises?"

"Please call me Tess," she said as she flipped open a rather heavy grimoire "There are two paths that you can chose to take, the first of which is a potion that tastes foul but it will cure you quicker or the second, though more time consuming has been recorded throughout all of these grimoires and has said to work almost 100% of the time, and I know how to perform the ritual."

"The choice is yours Captain, I just wish for you to be happy and free," Julian spoke softly as he felt the captains eyes lingering on him.

"But I do not wish to make this choice alone," she admitted as she squeezed his hands and peered over the large book in front of her.

"Then if you wish for my honest opinion, I feel we may have more success with the ritual. I feel in my bones that Tess can be trusted."

"I do not much like potions either. So it is agreed that we will go forth with the ritual?"

"It is."

"Then Tess, please, let us go forth and perform this ritual as quick as we can."

"Patience is a virtue my lady," Tess chuckled as she stood up and lead the lovers towards the back room of her cottage, where most if not all of her rituals were performed.

"It is not one we share," The Captain chuckled as they followed her into the back room with hearts full of hope.

***

As they entered the back room, they couldn't help but notice the way the prophetess had hung several bunches of protective herb bundles over the entry way of every door and ensured that the table was covered in West Draconda's finest silks. The smell of

cinnamon and Entraga – a scent only known people of
Elven blood and it was to the unknowing folk, an
uninviting smell of sickly sweet orchids, cloves and
deadly nightshade.

Julian raised an eyebrow at the scent but remained
quiet for he feared angering the prophetess and
destroying any chance they had at the ritual
succeeding.

"Captain, please remove your shirt and lay still upon
the table, arms at your side," the prophetess instructed
as she moved to search through her glass cabinets in
the hope of finding the correct elixir. The Captain
followed her instructions to the T, but she reached her
hand out to Julian and mouthed "Please don't leave
me here."

"I would not dream of doing anything like that," he
mouthed back and placed a gentle kiss to his lovers
temple.

"As for you Mr. Scott, I will need you to draw an
anaphora on your lady's stomach, and line the swell of
her breasts with the elixir before finishing off the
pattern with twin crescent moons and then I shall
prepare the spell."

The elixir was cold to the touch as Julian dipped two
fingers into the jar before standing beside his captain
and beginning to draw the anaphora in slow circles
before he allowed his hands to travel up her chest and
around the underside of her breasts. But the captain

couldn't help but stifle a small giggle. "What has tickled you my dear?" he whispered as he ran his fingers across the base of her neck before drawing a small crescent moon over her jugular.

"Only the fact that if this was under different circumstances, I would be welcoming your touch," she smiled coyly and only held in a gasp when she felt his piano player fingers along the side of her neck.

"My dear, you are insatiable," he chuckled, "I promise you will have your fair share of me when we are done. But right now I do not wish to anger our healer."

"Hmm, I suppose you are right. But will you promise me, that even if this gets ugly, you will stay with me?"

"You have my word and my heart," he said as he drew the last crescent moon on her forehead before pressing a quick kiss to the captains lips and turning to Tess to await further instructions.

"Ah you make me miss being young," she said as she watched the love grow and blossom between the two of them, "But alas, we must continue before nightfall comes again."

"I believe we have six or seven moons left before that final moon rises," The captain admitted as she gripped the table beneath her, more than ready to embrace the pain.

"Indeed we do, so let us begin," Tess spoke and rose her hands above the captains centre, "Jasha Kerin Tasia moon."

"That is elvish..." Julian muttered to himself as he whispered the translation to the captain "Villain of the haunted moon..."

"Bard, I know you are of elven blood, but you must refrain from interrupting the spell. You may explain all later but for now, allow me to work," she warned without opening her eyes.

"Sorry."

"Tec al forth, dash na allow se 12th moon ta rias. Willow's soul e a pure. Unlink ha leif from se Tome..."

"Tome?" The captain questioned as she looked to her bard with wide eyes and uneven breathe, but he simply shook his head and held her hand.

"Shh my love, I will translate all later," he mouthed, "You are safe."

"Ef he dies, kerin any cause, se cursa shall shatter, and thus free se Captain. He se plea Jasha Kerin Tasia Moon!" she said as she ran her hand above the captains torso, and as she did all the elixir drew into her and the room was filled with a light purple fog that dissipated out of the window within seconds of appearing. "The Spell is complete."

S. L. Coe

"What did she say?" The Captain said as she reached for her shirt and pulled it roughly over her head.

"May I translate?" he questioned as he came to embrace the captain from the side.

"You may."

He took a deep breath before he spoke and looked the captain in the eye "Before I say anything I just wish for you to know, that I was not aware that my people created this curse...Oh villain of the haunted moon, I call you forth, do not allow the 12th moon to rise. Willow's soul is pure. Unlike her life from that of Tome. If he dies, of any cause, the curse will shatter, and thus free the Captain. So hear my plea oh villain of the haunted moon."

"Elvish is far more terrifying when you do not know what is being said," the captain said as she rested her head on Julian's shoulder.

"I know my love; it was partially on purpose. At one point in our existence we wanted to be feared...a fat lot of use that was."

"I mean when you are in the presence of Tome, you are quite scary, albeit ethereal."

"Thank you..?"

"You're welcome," she chuckled as she lifted her head and placed her feet upon the cobblestones in attempts to stand, and yet she felt her knees were weak and she could not stand to take any more than a few steps.

"Captain, are you alright?" Julian asked as he broke her fall and placed his arm around her waist to keep her from falling again.

"She...you will be fine Captain," Tess confirmed as she placed her arm around the other side of the captain and guided her and Julian towards the small wooden bench that she had covered in orange cushions in the living room. "She will need to rest until the spell has ran through her body, she will be right as rain come this evening."

"Will I die if I fall asleep?"

"You will not die Captain, I specialise in healing and protective magic, you are safer here than out in the world for the next few hours. I shall find some tea for yourself and your gentleman bard" she said as she tucked a cover over the captains shoulders and let her rest on the bards thigh.

The rain steadily began to pour onto the windows as the wind picked up and howled out to the sky, it was clear the spell was taking affect. "You are so powerful," Julian whispered to the captain, his voice was soft and his brilliant blue eyes were filled with worry as he gently ran his hands through the captains long waves.

"Because the weather picked up?" she questioned, a hint of humour within her tired voice, but she did not move her head from where it laid in her lovers lap, rather she chose to draw nonsensical patterns with the occasional I love you into the thin material of his brown cotton trousers.

"Well that is a side effect of the spell, but no. That was not what I meant. You hold so much strength within you. You have survived trial after trial and never once batted an eyelid. You survived the torture of Tome and will be able to tell the tale soon. You...you make me whole and I could not be prouder of you, my Captain Willow Embers, who I thought just might have killed me back on that bandits ship all those moons ago if you were given the chance."

"Julian, firstly I would never have killed you, you enticed me, mind, body and soul since the moment I first laid eyes on you. But most of my tribulations would not have been lived through if I did not know you were trying to find me and stay by my side. I am not the only one to have survived Tome, you lost a part of you and are here fighting to bring an end to his reign of terror. Hell you saved an entire kingdom; you freed so many people from your fathers doing that I could not begin to shower you in enough praise. Perhaps that is why I love you so much. I am sorry we couldn't bring back your ears."

"I would look weird with them now anyway. I am just glad that you will be safe. I love you" he smiled softly, "Now rest my love, I shall be here when you awaken."

"And I promise you even if I do not have all the energy, I will let you enjoy tonight."

"My dear if you do not have the energy then our events can wait. It is no fun if both parties are not entirely there."

"Agreed," she mumbled as she began to drift into a gentle slumber, "I love you...I cannot wait to be your wife."

Although she mumbled about being his wife, Julian's heart couldn't help but skip a beat and cause his cheeks to flush pink, for he knew in his heart of hearts that she would one day be his wife, but he never believed that she felt the same. The worry in his heart sparked anew - despite his happiness – as he watched her fall asleep and shiver against the growing cold.

"Drink this, it will ease your nerves," Tess said as she handed Julian a large wooden mug of tea and settled herself in the seat opposite of him.

"How did you know to read the spell in elven?"

"Your mother was a wise lady and she taught me well -"

"Wait, you knew my mother?"

"Oh my dear boy, there is much you do not know, allow me to enlighten you..."

***

S. L. Coe

As the prophetess and the bard talked late into the early evening, the rain continued to drizzle down, a sure fire soon that the spell was almost as complete. The fireplace roared softly in the background as the kettle steamed quietly amongst the heat of the fire and despite the isle they were currently on, everything felt like home, like a future that was not too far away.

"So my mother really used to sneak out and tavern hop every night when she was twenty five?" Julian questioned through a surprised laugh and made sure that the blanket was still tucked up around the captains shoulders.

"Oh gods yes, she had the voice of an angel, something I'm certain she passed onto you. And by the gods, Pixie Isle was almost drunk dry the day she made sure to bless the land," she laughed as she clinked her mug against his and took a large swig of tea as if it were a tankard of ale. "Say, do you know what Pixie Isle is like this time of year?"

"Oh my lady, it is wonderful. I made sure that it was protect before I left, so anyone of good standing human, elf, orc or any other descent is welcome there. The Isle will know if you can be trusted – I mean, not you specifically, I know we can trust you – but in general, anyone dangerous is now prohibited from entering. Especially after the event with Tome." He sighed as he leant back on the sofa, and wished that he had his lute, for it was in a setting like this his creativity and inspiration seemed to thrive. "Do you think she'll ever be able to tell me what Tome did to her in the months she was gone?"

"As soon as the spell is complete and three months have passed, she should be safe to say. But I can tell you, it was nothing permanently damaging. Her soul told me as much."

He couldn't help but breathe a sigh of relief as he brushed her hair from her face and gently braided her hair with one hand, something that the captain had come to love about him, for despite the circumstances, he would always – always find a way to bring her great comfort. "And please do stop me if you find this next question inappropriate, but I must know, if the captain and I were to have a child...would it survive? Can elves and humans even have children? I know us elves are extremely fertile, but would it be possible?"

"Julian, I cannot speak from experience, as I was never as lucky with my husband to have had the opportunity to bear a child, but from my studies I have found that the chances of survival are at 95% - so you have a great chance of it working. And from what I have learned from you in this brief period of time, I know that you both will make great parents – even on the open sea."

"Why thank you good lady, I will be certain to tell you of the birth should it come to fruition."

"Are you planning my pregnancy already?" The Captain questioned as she brushed the sleep from her eye and snuggled up to Julian.

"Not as of yet my love, I was just enquiring to how likely a half elf, half human baby would be to survive, and talking about my mother again. She was far more wild then I first thought. Do you know she used to perform in taverns?" he beamed excitedly and looked towards the window where the rain has stopped and instead the stars had taken up residency in the deep blue sky above.

"Noo, your mother sounds like she was an amazing women. Remind me to visit her on the day of ghouls, I must meet her and thank her for bringing you to me."

"I shall remind you," he grinned, stood and folded the blanket before he placed it back down on the sofa below.

"It has been a pleasure to see you- " she yawned, "but I fear the spell has taken most of my energy for the day, so I must bid you adieu."

"That is perfectly fine my dear lady," Julian said and bent down to embrace Tess briefly before going towards the door.

"Thank you again Tess, you are welcome upon my ship anytime," she grinned, her honey brown eyes full of life again and held Tess tightly before letting go, with a quiet mutter of apology for squeezing her too tight and joined Julian by the door.

"Thank you both, I wish you well on your travels. Don't be strangers now!" She called as they went into the deep night.

"Stay safe!" They called back and walked hand in hand towards the tavern.

"How are you feeling?" Julian inquired as they walked as close as physically possible without falling over.

"Better. It's strange, I feel like I should be scared and running from the moon, but tonight I just feel so free and full of life. I...I finally have my life back."

"You look more alive, not that you did not before, it's just you look brighter...no happier," Julian rambled unable to find the right words amongst his happiness, "I'm just glad you feel like yourself again, and I look forward to seeing you thrive on that 12th full moon."

"Can we return to pixie isle on that 12th moon?"

"If that is what you wish, then it is my command," he said as he playfully bowed and placed a kiss upon her knuckles.

"You are such a lovesick fool," she laughed and embraced him as the moonlight bathed them in light.

"And you are much better?" he teased playfully and placed a soft kiss to her jaw, "Come, let us find ourselves neck deep in the taverns finest wine, I feel the crew might be missing us."

"Oh god, were they that loud before," she laughed and walked to the tavern with a skip in her step.

"Maybe not, but I'm sure the ale, wine and mead has their confidence soaring!" he cried as he ran after her and picked her up by the waist before twirling her around and kissing a line of playful kisses along her neck.

"Julian!" she playfully chided through a cry of giggles and span in his arms to press a passionate kiss to his lips, and it was like the world faded into a blissful silence. Her hands found the back of his shirt and pulled him towards her as he gently cradled her face and ran his thumb along her cheek. As the kiss grew deeper, they couldn't help but smile into it as they shared breath. "Gods I love you," she whispered as she rested her forehead on his and kept her eyes closed for a while.

"And I you my dear," he said as he ran his thumb along her soft lips, and gasped as she gently pulled it into her mouth and swirled her tongue around it before letting go. "My darling Willow, would you rather the tavern or our room first?"

"Hmm, that is a tough decision, but alas I must see my crew first. We will find ourselves time tonight."

"That promise, I shall make the utmost good on," he said and scooped her up in his arms, fully prepared to carry her to the entrance of the tavern, "We must also discuss the future."

"Indeed we shall my bard, indeed we shall. But first, I feel like we need some wine!"

"Then wine it is!"

The Bard and His Captain book 1: Damn Those Gods Inkpot

"Onward bard!" she cried, practically drunk of happiness.

"Aye - aye captain!" he laughed and walked to the tavern with her in his arms.

***

"There once was a young man who stowed away on our ship,

His tongue was as quick and as fast as his wit!

And his dick was as hard as a whip!

As our beautiful lady captain cried:

'oh fuck me bard, 'til I cannot sit!'

And it is with that, my friends.

The chorus will begin again'.

The crew chanted in tune to the banging of tankards, the stomping of several feet and the occasional peg leg. How they knew the events of what took place behind the captains quarters doors, was beyond them.

"Oh my darling crew, it was not me on my back" she laughed as she playfully clapped Thorian on the back as she sat down with two large glasses of mead and slid one over to Julian who turned to her with a devilish smirk.

"Maybe I will just have to reverse the roles tonight," he purred as he shot her a wink and took a swig of mead.

"You two are so gross!" Juliette jested as she pulled a face at the amorous couple, "get a room."

"Oh we plan to," The captain grinned as she met Julian's eyes, her own dark with an even mix of lust and love.

"We already have," The bard smiled back and placed his hand on top of the captains thigh, knowing just how weak she was to it. "But alas, we do have very serious matters to discuss."

"Shipping matters?" Thorian questioned, although his speech was slurred due to the amount of mead and ale he had consumed earlier.

But the captain simply shook her head and said, "No, personal matters between the bard and I, you and the crew are more than welcome to take the evening off. Tonight we may break the bedtime rule, and we shall see you all at the suns apex."

"Really?"

"Yes really, why are you so surprised?"

"Oh, it's just we never break the rules Captain, you're not going to marron us, are ye?" Thorian asked jokingly, although the nervous chuckle remained.

"Gods no, you are my friends as well as my crew, it just
so happens that a miracle was performed earlier
tonight, and after everything you have done for me
thus far, I figured you deserve some time off. And I do
not know how long I will take to wake in the morning."

"Thank the gods" Thorian muttered, before standing
and bowing to the captain, "Good night captain,
goodnight Julian."

"Goodnight my crew," the captain said and took the
bards hand and lead him towards the stairs as he
waved everyone a goodnight.

"So where do you want to start?" Julian asked as they
walked hand in hand into the room and lingered on
the threshold.

"I do not know, but I am wholeheartedly excited."

"How about we discuss the subject of marriage first?"
he said as he pushed the door to their room open and
scooped the captain up in his arms before he walked
over to the window seat and sat them both down so
that they were facing each other with only an inch or
two between them.

"Would you like to be married?"

"To you? There is no doubt about it. Would you like
to be married?" he said as he made sure to choose his
words cautiously to avoid jumping the gun.

"I would, you know, I had never dreamed of living a
life of solidarity for so long. Twenty four is a very long

time for a pirate – especially a female pirate captain – to remain unmarried or paired off at the very least. But I didn't wish to give my heart to just anyone. And thus I would be delighted to marry you!"

"Well twenty five is a grand old age to be alone, but I am grateful to have found you, and there is not enough words in any language to tell you all the ways I love you. I will find you the most perfect ring someday!"

"I am sure you will, but what about children? Parenthood is difficult anyway, but on the sea..."

"You know we do not have to conceive a child if you do not wish to," he said as he took the captains hands in his and rubbed small circles into the webbing of the thumb and forefinger.

"It's not that I do not wish to, it is more the fact I fear that I would not make a good mother."

"Nonsense, cap- Willow, you have shown great maternal instincts, if you can take care of a crew of at least 150 men and women if not more, then I'm sure our child will be no trouble at all. She will be the most loved child in existence."

"You wish for a daughter?"

"I do not mind what they identify as, but I have always pictured myself raising a daughter to follow the path of bardic – albeit with less emotional turmoil then I have experienced."

"Well you are in luck, for I myself have also wished to have a daughter – a queen of pirates if you would, you know if we did have a daughter what would you call her?" she said as she placed her hand over a non-existent bump.

"I would ideally like to name her after my mother, perhaps, Lilian-Meredith Scott."

"I like the sound of that, my mother's name was Lilian," she smiled softly as her mind swam with ideas of the future.

"What a coincidence!" he chuckled softly and caressed the captains cheek. She couldn't help but lean into his gentle touch and kiss his palm.

"Some of the world's greatest creations often are."

"I love you," he smiled as he pressed a gentle kiss to her lips and pulled her into his lap.

"I love you too," she mumbled against his lips, steadily losing herself in the feel of his hands.

"Would you rather marriage or the child first?" he purred as his lips left hers and travelled down her neck until he found the sweet spot that set her soul alight.

"Wedlock is nothing to fear, nor is it real. I do not care which comes first," she panted as she felt his teeth sink into her soft skin and leave a deep purple love bite that she would feel for days to come.

"Might we conceive tonight?" he questioned as he stood with her in his arms and she couldn't help but wrap her legs around his waist. The purposeful roll of her hips had him fighting the urge to buck his hips up to meet her.

"Julian, my love. Please stop fretting," she begged as she cupped his jaw and kissed him with so much passion that he felt drunk on love. "I want to make love with you. I want to have your child."

And it was with that, Julian pressed her against the nearest wall, the grip she had on his hips was enough to keep her stable between him and the wall. His heart thumped against his ribcage with such a ferocity he thought it might burst with all the love and adoration he had for her.

But as their lips danced against each other, the tension grew, and the captain could barely hold back her moans. Her hands found his hair and gave it a gentle tug as they parted for air. "The bed?" he questioned through quickened breath.

Her eyes were dark as they met his and she could barely form the words as she ran her hands down his chest, eager to strip him of all of his clothing. "I need you," she whimpered as she felt his hand graze her thigh, getting closer and closer to where she needed him most, but never touching her there. He couldn't help but smirk as he saw the frustration in his captains eyes.

"And you will have me, but tonight is about you," he
purred as he placed her gently on the bed and helped
her out of her shirt before settling his fingers at the
waistband of her trousers. "You are so beautiful" he
said as he admired the way she arched her back at the
slightest brush of his hands. He trailed his fingers in
the shape of anaphora on her stomach before he
traced the pattern up her chest and underneath the
swell of her breasts. One hand found her nipple, the
other he took into his mouth and slowly swirled his
tongue around the hardening bud.

Her breath caught in her lungs as she ran her hands
through his hair and yearned to feel his tongue
elsewhere. "Please, don't tease me," she begged as she
tugged his hair and tipped his chin up so that she could
look him in the eye.

"You don't want to be teased?" he questioned, his
voice low and seductive as he tilted his head, "Then
how about we make a game out of this?"

"A game?"

"Yes, if you can keep your hands above your head,
and resist the urge to touch me until I say so, then I
will not stop. But if you do not resist the urge, then I
will stop and leave you unsatisfied."

"But you said you never leave any partner unsatisfied!"
she cried, although she could not look him in the face
as her eyes drifted lower to the ever growing bulge in
his trousers.

"Ah my love, you did not let me finish," he said as he held her face gently in his hands, "I will leave you unsatisfied until you beg for more, and when you beg me, I shall take you from behind."

"May I ride you?"

"If you have any energy left after this, then be my guest," he purred as he leant forward and closed the gap between them until they fell back onto the bed, breathless and aroused. "Safe word?"

"Siren."

"Oh god, let us hope we do not have to use it," he laughed softly and helped the captain out of the remainder of her clothes, before undressing himself. A soft smile remained as his eyes ran over her body and admired every inch, every scar, every perfect imperfection, and in that moment he loved her even harder.

"Julian…" she sighed as she tried to keep her hands to herself and her gaze at his face, and yet the heat pooling between her thighs was becoming increasingly distracting.

"Captain," he said as he kneeled between her legs. He couldn't help but lick his lips as he ran his fingers through her lips and gathered her slick before bringing it to his lips and sucking them clean, "You taste delicious."

"Gods, I shan't last long if you do that ah-again!" she cried as she felt his tongue run along her sensitive slit until he found her clit and gently sucked it into his mouth as he slowly slid his fore and middle finger into her. It was with a great effort that the captain manged to keep her hands at her side. With his spare hand he gently pinched her nipple and smirked at the way her breath caught in her throat and turned into a whimper as she tried to call out his name.

"Do not worry love, I am not finished yet," he whispered as he moved to focus on the other nipple before adding a third finger and moving his tongue in a figure 8 motion, working her until her thighs began to shake around his head.

Her back arched off of the bed, and her hands twitched and went to move into Julian's hair, but as she saw him raise a challenging eyebrow, she reached for the soft sheets and gripped them so hard, she was sure they would rip. As she rolled her hips onto his hand, he curled his fingers against the spot that made her see stars. A deep moan rumbled in his throat and vibrated against her core as his cock begged for her touch. "Julian," she whimpered "I'm so close."

"I know darling," he said as he felt her clench around his fingers, and thus she spurred him on until she was trembling from the effects of her high. "Do you need to stop?"

"No, please don't stop," she plead as he leaned over her and pressed a kiss to her neck, right above her sweet spot. Her neck was covered in deep purple marks as Julian kissed his way to her lips, and when their lips connected it felt like the stars collided. Their souls were alight as she rolled her hips against him and moaned as the tip of his hardened cock just brushed her entrance.

"Fuck," he cursed under his breath and he had to steady himself on the bed frame as his whole body shivered and spasmed above her. He was desperate to feel her bounce on his cock, desperate to have her scream his name. "Gods I want to fuck you."

"Then fuck me, bard," she quipped, almost challenging him to fuck her into submission.

"As you wish, Captain," he said as he pumped his cock twice and spread a mix of her slick and his precum over the tip before he lined himself up with her entrance and entered her inch by glorious inch. Her eyes glazed over with lust as she adjusted to his size and said fuck it to the game as she hooked her legs around his waist.

Julian knew he wouldn't last long with this deeper angle, but by the gods she felt like heaven around him, as he held onto her hips and slowly thrust into her until all that filled the room was the sound of their gentle moans and the sound of skin against skin.

They could not care less if anyone heard, in fact he wanted them to hear just how well she took his cock. As he thrust into her, she ran her nails down his back

and called out his name desperately craving the edge
again, and then he stopped. "What did I say about
touching me?" he warned seductively, as he unhooked
her legs from around his waist and slowly pulled all of
the way out before he used both of his hands to flip
her over onto her hands and knees.

"Please sir," she begged as she laid forward on the bed
and rested her head on the pillow as she ground her
hips against the air begging for more.

"Sir?" Julian questioned as he bit his lip and closed his
eyes as he tried to postpone his high. When he
opened them again, they were darker than before and
his breath came out in soft pants as he ran his dick
along her slit, only teasing her with the tip, "Tell me
what you want".

"I want you to fuck me until you cum, and then I don't
want you to stop. I want to ride you; I want to have
your child."

"Then you wish is my command," he said as he
wrapped one hand around her hair and lined himself
up with her entrance again before he sank into her.
His hands roamed the gentle skin of her back and
moved around her hips until his fingers found her wet
sex. "Gods I burn for you," he purred in her ear and
caught her lips in a searing kiss as she began to grind
down on his cock until they found a steady rhythm that
had them both dangling on the edge.

His thrusts became sloppy as he felt his high growing ever closer, but that didn't stop him from stroking her clit and applying the smallest bit of pressure to get her to the edge, she couldn't help but clench around him as he gently pulled her hair until her back was pressed against her chest. "Are you sure you want me to finish inside you?" he asked breathless and red faced as a thin sheen of sweat covered the pair of them, and his hand ran gently along her neck.

"I want nothing more!" she cried as she felt the knot inside her stomach come undone and came around his cock.

"Then hold onto the headboard" he ordered as he let go of her hair and moved his hands so that they sat on her hips before he pound into her over and over again, spurred on by her elicit moans and whimpers. The knot in his stomach was rapidly coming undone, and just as he was about to cum – a knock at the door came.

A whimper left Julian's lips as he forced himself to stay still. He needed to cum, he needed to take care of the captain, but the knocking grew louder and they had not fastened the curtains. The captains eyes glazed over with lust and wanting as she rolled her hips and took him as deep as she could, gladly cock warming him. "Julian, I can't hold on for much longer."

"My lady, if you do that again, I will lose all control-" he said in a strangled moan, but his words were cut short when he felt the captain grind against him hard

and fast, practically begging for his cum. His whole
body shivered as an unhuman noise left his lips, his
hips spasmed and he began to thrust into her as hard
and as fast as he could whilst ensuring the two of them
would end satisfied. He leant forward so that his back
was against her front, and his lips were level with her
ear as they found a fast and intense rhythm that
worked for them. "Let them enter, I want them to see
just how well I fucked you"

"Come in," the captain said as she struggled to keep
her voice steady as she rolled her hips back onto him,
and in that move it was game over as Julian came deep
inside her. His whole body shook and his thrusts grew
faster until he was mostly spent, and it was only when
he felt the captain come around him did he catch his
second wind. "What...is...it?" she said as she turned
her flushed face to look at the intruder who stood with
a bottle of mead.

"I...I..." the intruder stumbled over his words as he
watched the amorous couple, slowly move apart and
switch places so that she now straddled the bard.

"Come on, we are very busy," the captain encouraged
the visitor, although her words were directed at the
bard who was incredibly hard already.

"I...ahem, I will come back later. It is not important,"
he said and slammed the door shut before running
down the stairs and to the lower level of the tavern.

S. L. Coe

The bard and the captain couldn't help but laugh as she laid on his chest until she got her breath back. "Who would have thought an intruder would have us coming undone so fast?" Julian jested as he ran his hand over the captains cheek and ran his thumb along her soft lips.

"Speak for yourself, you had me come undone twice before we even started," she chuckled as she reached behind her and lined him up with her entrance again. A shiver ran down her spine as she felt his cum being pushed back into her.

Julian whimpered at the over stimulation but he was more than happy to continue until she was satisfied, "Please do not stop."

"Oh my love, I don't plan to stop until the pair of us are entirely spent," she said as she slowly bounced her hips and placed her hands on his chest to keep him from moving too much.

"Gods, you feel amazing," he moaned as he bucked up into her, his hands found her hair and tugged gently as their lips crashed together in a searing kiss of passion. His tongue darted out and licked her bottom lip, asking for entrance which she gladly gave. Their tongues danced against each other, until they were begging for breath. As they parted, he sat up so that the captain stayed thrusting in his lap and he could attack her neck and breasts with kisses that he knew would leave her breathless.

"I...I can't hold on anymore," she said as her body began to shake. Their hands entwined at their side, and their lips were inches apart.

"Then do not, I am not far behind," he said as he closed the gap and thrust up into her until the pair were rushing to meet at the edge. And it was with a kiss that lead to him laying down on the bed with his arms around her hips, that they fell - in perfect synchronisation - over the edge together.

"By the gods that was amazing!" The captain sighed as she rolled off of Julian and laid by the side of him, holding his hand.

"You were amazing," he corrected as he traced nonsensical patterns along her arm, "Come let us clean ourselves up and then we can share a few moments together."

"I think that would be best, but I do not think I can walk."

"You are not the only one," he laughed softly as his legs wobbled when he tried to stand, "Put your arm around me and we shall walk over to the basin together."

"And if we fall?"

"Then that is just a few more love fuelled bruises we will have to explain to the crew," he offered as they walked over to the basin, where two wash cloths sat waiting.

As they got themselves clean, something new lingered in the air.

Something far more hopeful and exciting, as they were about to embark on their new journey together.

"How long do you think it would take us to tell if it worked?" the captain questioned as they started to re-dress each other in fresh clothing that they had found in the draws of their room.

"That is something I hadn't thought to ask Tess, but I imagine it is just like a usual human pregnancy."

"Or Elven."

"Perhaps, an Elven one only lasts a month more," he thought aloud as they sat side by side on the bed, with practically no space between them, "Was I too rough on you?"

"No, why would you think that?" she said as she wrapped an arm around his waist and edged closer to snuggle into his side.

"I just wanted to make sure that you enjoyed it, I am not very used to being in control – in the bedroom at least."

"Julian my love, look at me. I loved every single second of it, and I love every part of you both inside and outside of the bedroom. Was it good for you?" she said as she rubbed small circles on his back and played with a few stray strands of his hair.

"It was something else entirely, I did truly love all of it, as I love you," he smiled softly and pressed a kiss onto her forehead. "Thank you."

"You have nothing to thank me for."

"I know, but you were phenomenal," he said as the brightness returned to his eyes and his smile grew brighter.

"Me? Julian, your moves were far more impressive. If I had been a virgin, your tale would have gone down in history."

"Aw, does that mean you will not tell the world of our escapades?" he teased playfully as he began to braid the captains hair.

"Maybe I will, but for now I will keep it to myself – I burn for you. I love you more than stars themselves."

"As do I you, more than words can express," he smiled softly as he stood and offered his hand to the captain, "We should properly go see what our intruder wanted."

"I hope we didn't scar him too badly."

"Scar him? Nay my lady, I reckon we inspired him."

Chapter 17: To the cavern of death isle, an accident waiting to happen.

Inspiration and scarring could go hand in hand as the poor intruder sat against the wooden pillar, with a bottle of mead in one hand and something small in his pocket in the other. "Oh Christ it's you two!" he said as he immediately released the small object and stood to look at them sheepishly.

"I told you we'd inspire him," Julian said as he flashed the captain a knowing smile and wrapped his arms around her shoulders.

"Inspire him? Julian, the poor man's trembling," she laughed before schooling her expression and taking on the captain persona "What is your name?"

"William, William Jonson," he said as he clutched the bottle tighter. "I was sent by your crew to warn you of the ghosts."

"The Ghosts?" Julian questioned and raised a curious eyebrow as he was a big believer in the supernatural.

"Yes, the ghosts of loved ones are said to linger in the caverns, the underground city of Death Isle!"

"But why would the crew need to warn us?" The captain asked as she looked over to the crew who were either sharing tales of the sea, or drunk asleep on the table.

"They said they saw the image of fallen family members. Including your parents."

"As in whose parents?"

"Both of yours. Just your mothers, they said they wanted to protect your souls should you run into that nasty rat faced man."

"You know Tome?" Julian asked as he eyed the man sceptically – for he was unsure if he – the man – was one of Tome's spies.

"Know him? I despise him! He hunted us down when the war was at its worst."

"Say what was your last name again?"

"Jonson, why does it matter? He is not here; he is not allowed to step foot on the island."

"Because, I believe your grandfather may have been a patron at the tavern of Pixie Isle," he said as he kept his voice low enough so that only William and the captain could hear him.

"He was! James was his name, but he died a couple of weeks ago, hence why I am here on the week of ghostly risings," he explained as he offered the mead to the captain first, who politely declined and then to Julian who did the same, no longer in the mood for drinking. Instead, his mind began to swirl with worry.

Would Tome find them here? Would he be lingering at the dock? Does he have the strength to bring an end to Tome – and if he does what would the captain say after what they just did?

But Julian was soon snapped out of his thoughts as the captain lightly tapped on his chest, just over his heart, "Hey, are you alright?"

"Sorry, Tome got in my head again," he sighed as he looked to the ground unable to find the energy to fake an 'I'll be okay' smile.

"Do you need some air?"

"Air and a large tankard of wine," he muttered under his breath.

"Wait outside, I shall bring it to you," and with that she walked over to the bar and got herself and Julian a drink.

Julian however had walked straight ahead from the tavern and went to sit with his legs in the sea as he watched the stars, but he was not alone for Thorian, Juliette, John and the Captain all brought their tankards out with them and sat on the dock next to him.

The Captain laid her head on Julian's shoulder. "You know you're never going to be alone right. And if tome ever comes for you, just know we'll all be waiting for him."

"As long as you guys do not give your life in the process, I think I could live with that," he said, relieved that at long last his mind was able to fall silent.

"I make no promises there, you protected us, we will do the same for you," Thorian piped up as he raised his tankard and leant so that they could all meet in the middle "To the crew, the captain and new friends."

"Aye- Aye!" they cheered and clinked their tankards before taking a big swig, more than ready to drink the night away.

But as Julian raised his tankard to his lips, his eyes pricked with unshed tears that he tried to blink back.

"Bard, are you alright?" Juliette asked as she watched him look out towards the towering cathedral.

"Oh, yes, I shall be fine," Julian lied as he brushed his hand over his face and schooled his expression before taking a rather large swig of wine.

"Julian..." The captain spoke softly as she shuffled a little closer to him, "Be honest with us."

"But I do not wish for you to see me as someone weak."

"We would never think that you are far stronger than anyone of us," The captain promised as she placed her hand upon his leg and gave it a gentle squeeze.

His voice was horse as he spoke, desperately trying to hold back his tears, "Do you...do you ever wish that you had taken a different path in life?"

"How do you mean?"

"Sometimes I just think what would have happened if I had stayed at the castle for just an hour longer, if I had just stayed to hear what they had to say, they would still be here and I...I would still..."

"Is it about your mother?" The captain questioned as she traced the pattern of a fern leaf onto the back of his hand, it was something that he had confided in the captain long ago.

"It is more than that my love. It is ghosts night, fifteen years to the day is the day I lost everything to Tome," he said as a single tear slipped down his cheek "I lost my faith, my respect, my ears, my mother. The day I was trapped beneath that cathedral was the day my mother took her last breath...and by the time I had gotten home, bloodied and bruised, he had already defiled her twice and tossed her in the ground. No coffin. Just the earth and its creatures."

The captain and her crew mates said nothing as they listened and allowed him to speak. Instead they placed their tankards to the side and moved so that they could all be close to the bard.

"I am just terrified that he will find me again and make me as powerless as the day he robbed everything from me. I am terrified that he will come for you," he cried as he looked at the captain, his face full of tears as she stared back with watering eyes, "I am terrified that he will come for them when they are old enough to exist outside of you."

"Julian, my love, please hear me when I say you are safe. I will keep you safe, and they shall remain untouched – even before they can exist outside of me. I made you a promise, I will honour it even in my dying breath."

"But what happens if I am not good enough to be a father? I do not want to turn out like my own."

"And-"

"And you shan't," His mother's voice whispered in the wind.

"Mother?" he questioned as he wiped his ever falling tears from his cheeks, "I cannot see you."

"You will in time my dear sweet child," she said as she made the wind blow gently through his hair. "You have picked the most wonderful bride, thank you captain for taking care of my son."

"You are welcome Meredith," The captain said as she curtsied in the direction of the voice before she took her place next to Julian.

"You are nothing like your father, he was a vile and cruel man who did unspeakable things to you. And I am sorry that I could not protect you from him nor Tome. But you are not them, you are kind, you are loving and sweet, and I know you would give all you had to protect those that you love. And that is how I know you will make an excellent husband and father, so do not worry" she smiled and used what little energy she had to make the wind lovingly embrace her son, "You are in safe hands. And I shall see you when ghost night falls. I love you my little lark."

"I love you too, Mother," he smiled and waved into the air as he felt his mother's spirit fade into the night, and his heart piece itself together. New tears slipped down his cheeks as his smile grew brighter.

"Are these good tears?" Thorian asked as he blew his nose into a hankie and then offered it to the bard, who through a tearful laugh declined.

"They are very good tears, I thought she died in pain. I thought I would never get to hear her voice again, but now I know that I can continue this fight," he said and opened his arms to embrace his captain and crew, "Come here."

And by gods did they as wrapped their arms around the bard and squeezed each other tight, almost as if they wanted to knit their lives together, and in a world like this, they would take what they could find.

***

The caverns were cold but full of life as the market stall holders began to open up their shop for business, and the silversmith prepared his smithy for the long day ahead. The usual sound of dancers who held bells on their ankles and made sure to ring them as loud as they could – so much so that the sound bounced off of the cavern walls.

"How did I not know this place existed?" Julian cried as he ran over to a stall that sold countless tins of lute lacquer – his own lute banged against his back as a smile danced across his lips.

"Careful bard, any faster and your wonderful hair would be covered in lute lacquer," Thorian laughed as he leant on his axe and watched as the bard compared each tin and looked towards his lute for conformation – almost as if it would speak the answers to him.

"Maybe, but at least then it would be half off," he jested as he dug into his coin purse in search of the right coins to pay the vendor.

"It's nice to see you happy again," Thorian said as he wandered further down the cavern until he came to the silversmiths who was still preparing his metal.

"What do you mean?" he questioned innocently as he leant against the wall and gently strummed the lute in a tune that he had been working on over the course of the week.

"It just ever since we mentioned *him* you haven't seemed like yourself, neither has the captain, but it is nice to see you both happy and yourselves again," he said as he nodded over to the captain who stood in front of a broken mirror and tried to determine which corset to buy.

"I know, and I am truly sorry that I have made you all miserable, but now I feel as though the wind is blowing in a better direction and now I just I need to find the correct ring," he said as he looked over the silversmiths pre-made rings.

"A ring?"

"Hmm, for the captain," he nodded as he held one up to the candlelight but decided he didn't like the way the silver sheened.

"What's the occasion?"

"I wish to marry her, I do not know if we were successful in creating a child, but I am choosing to remain hopeful and by the end of the year, once her curse is lifted for certain, I wish to ask for her hand in marriage."

"How would you do it?" Thorian asked as he came up beside the bard and went through a small section of rings that he put aside to show him later.

A bright smile danced across Julian's lips as he thought back to the first night they spent together all the way back at Anya's tavern, "I think I would do it in ballad. It was what first drew her attention to my performance, when we had only known each other a couple of day, I performed a song about a beautiful pirate captain who had become my muse and someone who I wished to write more songs about. And so I figured, a new ballad would be the perfect way to go."

"Julian, you are a true gentleman and hero," Thorian said as he cleared his throat and held up the rings to him. But there was only one that stuck out to him, and that was a thick silver ring that held the crest of an anchor and a lute on the signet – and he knew in that moment that it was the one.

"Thorian you are a genius! Thank you!" He beamed as he took the ring and ran up to the silver smiths smithy, desperate to engrave the inside with the date in which they met.

"Careful bard, you're going to do yourself injury!" the gruff silver smith spoke as he patted the sparks out of his thick black beard.

"I am sorry sir, but I need to have this ring engraved, it is for my partner," he said as he looked over to his shoulder only to see his captain staring back at him, with love in her eyes, a soft smile on her lips and her hand on her belly. He waved over to her, but soon returned his attention to the silver smith, but not before he silently asked Thorian to distract her, lest she find out about the surprise.

"The Captain of the Black Bess?"

"You know my Captain?"

"Know her? She is my sister, I believed her to be dead after the first effect of the curse," he said as he looked over to the dwarf and the captain who sat on barrels discussing their next adventure.

"Did you not go looking for her? You know she is an excellent captain and an even greater woman."

"I tried, but our mother said it was futile and when I did go searching behind our mothers back, she banished me to work in the caverns of death isle, and this is where I have remained for the past sixteen years."

"But pray tell, did you not think to find her body regardless of your mothers wishes, or would you rather have left her body to rot had she met her untimely demise?" The bard demanded as he stepped into the silver smith and held the unforged ring tightly within his grasp.

"Bard – you greatly misunderstand, I did not mean to cause such harm, I only-"

But alas the silver smiths words were cut short as Julian held his hand up and looked the silver smith in the eyes, his own filled with fierce determination, "I am the king of West Draconda, and what you intended to do does not mean much to me, it is what you did that does. And the fact that the Captain does not speak of you, speaks volumes about your significance in her life. So please, unless you are willing to engrave the ring with the date in which we first met, then please do not attempt to interfere with the captains life."

"My lord, I shall have the ring completed and sent to your temporary residence and then I shall be out of your hair for good."

"Good, and what will be the cost of the ring and said engravement?"

"I shall ensure that it is on the house, regardless of my time," He said as he took the ring from the bard and placed it upon his smithy, more than ready to get to work.

"Thank you, good day, good sir," he said and descended down the stairs and towards the small corner in which the captain and Thorian sat, happily discussing the future voyages and events.

"Did you get the thing?" Thorian questioned as he gave him a subtle wink and moved his head in the direction of the silver smith who was frantically smithing away.

"I did, he said he will deliver it to the tavern as soon as he can..." and whilst the bards heart was in his words, his mind was not – for out the corner of his eyes he spotted the tell-tale signs Tome's bright blond hair and the dagger which he had previously used to remove the tips of the bards ears – glistened in his hand. "Please, excuse me," he said as he moved as quickly as he could to follow the villainous heathen through the caverns tunnels.

"Julian!" The Captain cried as she reached for his arm and pulled him towards her, a fiery determination in her eyes, "What the hell are you playing at?"

"Tome is here. He will kill all of us if he sees you are alive, there are enough eyes on you and us as it is!" He said as he tried to pull himself free from the Captain, a plea of forgiveness in his eyes, "I will explain all, but please go back to the tavern. I cannot have more blood on my hands than I already have."

"I am not leaving you; I am not allowing you to walk into the lion's den and expect to come out the other side alive."

"My Captain, you have to understand I am not doing this to be selfish, I am doing this to protect you – your brother the silver smith, is here, searching for you. And if Tome is here, that means it is game over-".

"Bard, I do not have a brother," she spat as she narrowed her eyes and looked towards the silver smith who stood with the ring in hand, and looked towards where the captain, Julian, and Thorian all stood.

"Then who is that?"

"I do not know, but if Tome is here then I suspect that it is not someone of good conscious."

"Right," Julian said as he took a harsh breath and looked to the sky before focusing back on the captain, desperately willing for the memories of his torture to remain at bay.

"Julian, look at me!" she commanded and cupped his face so that he could only focus in on her, "We will bring an end to him together, whether we end up dead or not I do not care, I will not have him continuing to terrorise you nor anyone else."

"I want revenge for everything he did to my people, for everything he did to me, and most importantly everything he has done to you. I will make sure that his final moments are full of nothing but suffering," he warned as his voice filled with venom and a powerful fistful of red and purple elven magic – that sparked with lightening – crackled in the bards hands. His eyes seemed to glow in the heat of the cavern, and the captain knew in this moment that it was now or never. It was fight or die trying.

"Julian, take me with you and I promise, he will suffer with every breath he takes" she said as she placed her hand on his wrists and slowly passed an ounce or two of her magic to him, as a caution and protection. "Please..."

He looked towards his feet and the captain in a futile effort to convince himself to take her back to the tavern, but as he swallowed his pride, there was only one answer that was obvious. She had to be with him, they were a package deal. Now and forever. And it was with a lump in his throat and his heart pounding against his ribcage that he took the knee for her, and held her hands within his, "You may come with me, but on one circumstance, and I was going to wait until I had the ring in hand – but I fear in asking for the ring, I may have placed everyone's life in jeopardy – but if we are to complete this suicide mission together, then please my darling Willow, would you do me the most extraordinary honour of being my wife?"

"My god Julian, you are a wordsmith and half," she beamed as she squeezed his hands before parting them so that she could embrace him with all her might, "Of course I will!"

His breath left his lungs as she squeezed him so tight that it took him a moment to realise that she had said yes! "I love you Captain Willow Embers," he beamed as he captured her lips in a swift but tender kiss.

"And I love you King and Bard Julian Scott," she grinned as she pulled herself away from the kiss and took his hand in hers, "Thorian I need you to return to the tavern and ensure all of the crew are safe. Take them on the passage to the cottage, and we shall find you once we are safe. Promise me you shan't come looking for us?"

"I promise, but Captain, Bard, please do not leave us without a leader. Without our friends."

"I cannot make any promises, but we shall find you when dawn has risen again." Julian said as he placed his free hand on the dwarfs shoulder and gave a supportive squeeze before he turned to the captain and held her hand tight. "Now we run!"

Chapter 18: A child trapped in the tunnel.

As they ran through the caverns tunnels, the path became more and more convoluted. Tome's hideous laughter bounced off of the walls and ricocheted into Julian's head – and thus rendered him speechless to the captains questions. He ran with his head down and his hand gripping the captains, determined to find that villainous ratcatcher before he escaped their grasp again.

"Oh my, my, watch how the king runs!" Tome taunted and used magic to elevate the sound of his voice, "It's so pitiful, you know you'll never catch me."

"Fuck you," was all that made it past Julian's lips as he turned the corner, prepared for whatever may jump out of the alcoves, and yet nothing appeared. Or at least, nothing that Julian could see. But it was in the darkness that he felt the cold rush of wind that his mother had brought with her earlier. He silently willed her away, for he did not wish for her to see what he was about to do.

"JULIAN!" his mother's voice bellowed above him, it was shrill and full of fear as she dropped a golden dagger onto the floor before him, "Take this!"

"But that, that was the dagger you said would bring around the end of the elven kingdom," Julian said as he bent down to collect the dagger before pulling himself and the captain into a small alcove.

"It is, but what I did not tell you is that, that dagger is capable of bring an end to the one who places the elven kingdom in the most danger. Use it on Tome and he shall no longer roam this earth."

"Mother, are you absolutely certain this will work?"

"Indeed I am, I had Lilian help me remodel the blade so that his soul would forever be trapped in the underworld."

"Wait you know my mother?" The Captain questioned as she stepped towards the voice and began to take the knee.

"Please Willow do not bow to me, I am not a queen anymore. But yes, your mother and I were very close when we were younger. I believe she shall be paying a visit soon enough. But we do not have enough time to discuss it now, run Tome approaches!" His mother warned before dissipating into thin air and guiding them along a secret tunnel that would lead directly to Tome.

"Are you going to use the dagger?" The Captain asked as she readied her sword.

"I hope I do not have to. I wish to use my own until he is at the brink of death."

***

Julian's eyes narrowed as he wandered down the tunnel, no longer holding the captains hand. Instead he held onto his mother's dagger in his left, and in his right elven magic crackled and fizzed, just waiting to explode.

"Show yourself you pitiful coward!" Julian spat as he shoved wooden door after wooden door open until he came to a locked chamber. "Where has your bravado gone, hm, I thought you would have yearned for this opportunity to strike me dead?!"

"Julian..." The Captain whispered as she stood beside him, remnants of her magic trying to spark to life as her eyes stopped and laid transfixed onto a small child. The child was no older than four and yet she had blood dripping from the tips of her ears, and Julian's breath caught in his throat as he laid eyes on the child.

The bard immediately dropped to his knees in front of them, and dropped his blades, before gently placing his hands onto their shoulders, "My darling, can you hear me?" he questioned as he wiped a tear from their cheek.

She nodded but pointed to his lips and then pointed to her ears and shook her head. She could not hear him, but she knew how to read his lips.

"Okay my darling, we can work with that. Do you know who did this to you? Can you draw the letter in the air?"

S. L. Coe

She nodded and with a shaky hand she drew a small 'T' in the air. And in that moment he knew. He knew that Tome must be brought to his knees and be made to pay. It took everything within him to keep from screaming out in deep sealed agony. "Thank you, I need you to listen carefully to me, okay? I need you to run as fast as those legs can carry you and find the nearest tavern, our crew will be waiting for you. They will protect you, tell them that Julian Scott and Captain Willow Embers sent you, and they will keep you safe, as will the sprits in this cavern." Julian explained and opened his arms to embrace the small child, "Inviseque" he muttered and allowed the child to run into the tunnels, protected by invisibility until either his mother's soul found her or she found the tavern.

And whilst the child was gone, he did not move. He could not move as he stared transfixed on the spot where she stood, silent hot tears spilled down his cheeks.

"Oh Julian, come here," The Captain spoke softly as she embraced him, and ran her hands through his hair, desperate to ground him, "You did the right thing."

"I know...but what happens if we cannot bring an end to Tome and the same thing that happened to that child, happens to ours! I could not live with myself if that were the case," he cried as he buried his head in the crook of the captains neck.

"And it won't. Like you said, the crew will protect them."

"I broke one of your rules," he gasped as he pulled away to look at her, a sincere apology lingered in his eyes, "I am so, so sorry my love."

"Julian, we broke my rule," she said as she took his hand and placed it upon her stomach, "I know it is early days yet, but I can feel my body changing to accommodate our child. So we would be sailing with a child regardless."

"So you're not going to maroon me?"

"I would never maroon you," she reassured him and wiped his tears before pressing a gentle kiss to his forehead.

"Thank you Willow," he whispered and pulled her into a warm embrace, "But promise me, you will not look at me differently for what is about to happen to Tome."

"My love. My bard. I cut a woman's tongue out simply because she tried to kill you, so I shall not be standing at the side-line when we bring an end to him. Nor shall I look at you differently for doing what needs to be done, will you me?"

"Not at all," he confessed and took his blades from the ground before he hauled himself and the captain to their feet, "I love you."

"I love you too, you shall make a wonderful father," she smiled softly as she entwined their hands and looked towards the door, "Now we shall end this once and for all!"

"Prepare to meet the Queen of the underworld, Apollo Tome," he spat and shoved the door to his chamber open.

Chapter 19: To die by The Captains hands, is something he does not fear. The Bards is another story entirely.

When the door swung open the rat faced man sat in the dark laughing to himself, just as a mad man would. In his hand he held an elven long sword that glittered with harmful magic. "At last, we meet again," he said, his voice like velvet venom. "Do you like my art?"

"Art? Art! Those a child's ears, you are one sick bastard if that is what you consider art," Julian hissed through gritted teeth, desperately holding back his rage as he used his magic to highlight the furthest corner of the room. "What was the purpose of that? Why maim a child if you wished to get to us?"

"Because my wonderful bard," he purred as he stood and dragged one slimy finger along Julian's jaw line – bile rose in his throat as he pulled his face away from Tome's touch – "I know of what is to come. And I wanted to give you a preview just in case you thought you could escape me."

"I will end you," Julian spat as he headbutted the villain and drew his sword more than ready to strike until he heard the captain gasp and clench at her stomach, "Captain! What are you doing to her?"

"He's trying to kill her," the captain gasped as she fought to withhold a scream.

And Julian saw red as he stormed towards Tome until he had him pinned to the wall by his throat, "Leave them out of this. They play no part in your pitiful game. You want to fight someone? You truly wish to leave someone dead? Then that person is me. Leave my wife and child out of this," he threatened and squeezed the bastards throat until he was almost gagging for air.

"Oh my, who knew the bard would be jumping the gun," he taunted and relaxed his hand until the door swung open, "She may leave."

"Captain?" Julian questioned as he kept a hand on Tome's throat and looked over to the captain – fear threating to spill over the surface.

"I'll be fine," she whispered although her voice wobbled as she fought to keep the tears falling down her cheeks.

"Please leave me," he plead, "Get to the healer, and I promise you I shall find you; I want you both to live even if I do not."

"I cannot leave you!"

"You can, I need you too!"

"But what if you die?"

"Then I shall find you as a ghost and stick by your side! But if you die, then I will be sure to follow you."

"Julian..."

"Willow, please! Leave me."

"Promise me you'll stay alive," she cried as the tears flowed freely down her cheeks and whilst she yearned to stay, yearned to hold onto him, she knew it was futile – he was right. There was no reason to risk two lives just to spare the one.

"I promise you; I shall find you again," he said as he met her eyes, his own tears wet his lashes as he willed for her to go. "Run and don't stop running until you are safe!"

"I shan't. I estu."

"You are always full of surprises," he smiled and nodded, finally able to let her run free.

And run she did as the door slammed shut.

And thus the villain was trapped with the vengeful bard.

"Now it is time you pay," he said as he squeezed Tomes throat once moor before dropping him so fast that he his knees cracked on the cobblestone floor. A swift kick came to Tome's gut before the Bard crouched down and looked the villain in the eye, "Before I kill you, tell me why you are so hell bent on destroying everything this world has to offer."

"Why do you care, you'll only kill me anyway," he spat as blood dripped down his chin and he reached for the bard who simply batted his hand away and stood above his victim.

"Because unlike you, I like to understand the traitors reasoning. I will ensure that your tale is told through out west Draconda, and once it is heard, I shall ensure you that your head will be stuck on a spike a paraded around the continent until it becomes nothing but a skull to feed to the wolves. Now speak, lest you wish to lose your tongue," Julian's eyes grew dark with hatred as he stared down at the man who had taken everything from him, his magic began to spark to live again.

Tome's eyes went wide and he held his hands in front of his face as he grovelled "Okay, Okay, you win, I shall talk!"

Julian simply grabbed the villain by the hair and pulled him to his feet before he shoved him into the chair with extremely little care as to where he landed. "Why do you go after children? Does it give you a power trip knowing they are so innocent compared to you?"

"I never had a childhood, bard. Why should they be so lucky, you elven lot are a pitiful bunch, caring for children and elders over those underdogs that matter."

"Underdogs? Is that truly what you believe yourself to be? You are nothing but pure unadulterated evil and if you shall not tell me your truth, then I shall pluck it from you" he hissed and clapped his hands onto either side of the villain's head – his eyes shut as he dug through Tome's mind. Visions of his victims torture and the torching of pixie isle filled Julian's mind. "I am not a villainous person by nature, I sing songs and perform in taverns, I do my utmost to save who I can, and yet there is no saving you."

"Oh I do not wish to be saved," he said through gritted teeth and pushed the bard off of him, a dagger of his own in his hand, and he marched towards the bard until he was close enough to sweep his legs out from underneath him.

Julian gasped for breath as he hit the cobblestones, his dagger skidded across the room, and he could do nought but shield his face as Tome attempted to slash at him. His blood boiled from within and his eyes glowed against the dark – the once brilliant blue had now been replaced with an icy white and his skin was covered in ancient elven runes. "I am a king. I will not bow to you," Julian said through gritted teeth and gripped Tome's wrist and pushed with all of his might until he heard a deafening crack followed by an agonising scream. He knew his reputation would shatter once the world caught word of what he had done, but he could not care less as his magic ran through his veins and down to his hands where the red and purple mist filled with lightening.

"You killed thousands of my people. You threatened my kingdom. You tried to kill the woman whom I love. You came for my family" he spat as he threw blast after blast of electric daggers into Tome's side, "And you think that I am going to allow you to leave this cavern alive, oh no, you are sorely mistaken."

"The same could be said for you, I wonder what will run out first, your magic or your life force."

"Oh much has changed since I was last here. Because I am not trapped with you, you see, you are the one who's trapped with me," he laughed bitterly and dove his dagger into the villains' groin and pulled it down until it almost reached his genitals.

The villain screamed and cried out, unable to find the words to torment the bard further. And yet, as he arched his back, he only caused the knife to dig deeper.

Julian smiled wolfishly down at the villain and pinned his head to the side and yanked the dagger out of his groin before slashing it over Tome's ear. His ears laid at his side and all he could do was cry. "It's not so fun when you are on the receiving side," he spat and kicked them away and allowed for Tome to stand.

The glow of Julian's eyes died down and his eyes returned to their usual blue but the fire in his soul remained. "Come, fight me like a man," he encouraged as he moved his index and middle finger in a come at me motion, a wicked grin on his face.

"You will lose," Tome threatened weakly and stood, blood dripped down his face and dripped towards his eyes. He became the human epitome of evil. And

Julian knew in that moment he would have to fight tooth and nail if he wished to make it back to the captain alive.

A fist came barrelling towards the bard and before he even had time to react, it had settled itself in the bards stomach, over and over again until he was certain he would lose his lunch.

"Fuck you," the bard muttered and pushed off of the wall and ran towards him, until his fist crashed into the underside of his jaw, the ancient elven runes burned into the villain, and he hissed in pain, unable to move.

Tome looked at the bard as he was stuck to the spot – frozen by fear. "Come on then, take your best shot. KILL ME!"

"Oh no, it is far more satisfying for you to kill yourself," he growled as he used his magic to place the golden dagger his mother had gifted him in his enemy's hand, and through the use of ancient elven magic – that was considered to be forbidden amongst many – guided the dagger to his throat. "Any last words?"

"Fuck you-"

And yet before the villain could finish his sentence, the dagger drove itself into the bastards throat and set the body alight, blood gargled in his throat as he tried to scream. And yet as the fire burned and the text began to remove itself from the bards skin, all Julian wanted to do was scream and cry.

He was free, but at what cost? His mind was spiralling as Tome's body drifted into the underworld.

Julian pressed his head to the cold concreate wall as he finally allowed all of his barriers to crash around him, a scream ripped from his throat as his legs gave out from beneath him. The sound echoed around the tunnels, and he was certain he could be heard by the market, but in this moment of weakness, he could not care less. All of his broken pieces fell apart and knitted themselves together over and over again. Memories of his own torture, of his own village burning, of his captain in pain flooded his mind, he couldn't find the breath to fill his lungs as anxiety and fear washed over him. He laid in a pool of his own blood as every ounce of magic he once had left him, he looked like himself again (even if the ancient runes remained), and yet it was his heart that lingered in two places – he was free but he could not heal – not yet.

His mouth was dry as he cried, and yet all he could whimper was the captains name.

"Julian…" his mother's voice called out as the sound of gentle footsteps hit the cobblestones.

"Mother?" he asked softly as he slowly opened his eyes – half expecting to see Tome standing before him.

"It's me. You are safe my darling," she promised as she finally allowed herself to manifest into this plane of existence. As she spoke she brushed her sons hair from his face, "Are you alright?"

But before Julian could get his words out, the vomit rose in his throat and shuffled away from his mother before he allowed it to project out of him. He sat with his knees to his chest and wiped his lips before he looked towards his mother and spoke, "Did I do the right thing?"

"Darling, you did everything right. If you had not done this, then I believe the captain would have."

His heart pounded in his chest as his eyes widened and he rose to his feet ready to run down the cavern tunnels, "My captain! Did you see her? Did she recover? Did she make it to the healers...our child? Did she die?"

"Julian, Julian, Julian, listen to me," his mother said as she grabbed his shoulders and turned him to face her, "She will be fine. Last I saw, she was inside the healers. The baby is safe, as is she. I shall come with you to find her, but first we must attend to your wounds."

"My wounds matter not when she is out there, alone," he gasped as he applied pressure to his stomach, in hopes he would have enough magic to heal himself, and yet nothing happened. A single tear slipped down his face as he cursed under his breath. "My hands hurt," he laughed bitterly as he held them to his chest.

"Come my son, I shall heal you."

"Are you sure I am alive?"

"I am more than certain," she chuckled at his question and ruffled his hair before attending to his wounds.

"And you're certain, she is alive and well?"

"Julian..."

"I am sorry mother; I am just worried to the point I am afraid I may lose my lunch again."

"We will find them both well."

"I truly hope so."

***

"Bard! Bard! Are you all right?" Thorian asked as he held onto the Bards arm, but alas Julian flinched at the touch and held his arms to his chest, breathing shallowly o keep the pain at bay.

He couldn't look at the dwarf before him, he did not wish for his friends to see the pain within his eyes, "I'll be fine," he muttered and kept his eyes on the exit of the cavern "Did you see the captain pass through here or a small child by any chance?"

"I have not," he said as he shook his head, panic written deep within his eyes, "Is she okay?"

"I do not know. I sent the child to seek out the crew, and the captain to the healer...but if she has not passed through here, then. Oh gods."

"What is it?"

"Please, excuse me," he said as he bolted for the exit of the cavern, he did not care to hear everyone calling after him. He paid no attention to his gaping wounds; he did not care what stalls he bumped into on his way out. All he needed, all he wanted to know was if his captain lived.

His heart felt as though it was about to burst as he saw the light of the tunnel, and his mind spun with a million questions – *"did she make it out alive? Did their child survive? Did the small elven four year old make it to the tavern? And if the answer to all of those questions is no, then what happens then?"* He could not think straight, and if he was being honest with himself, he did not wish too.

Because in doing so, meant potentially coming to terms with the fact that the love of his love and his unborn child would be meeting death thanks to his own hands.

Chapter 20: Oh my captain, my captain.

You breathe at last!

By the gods, the bard wanted nothing more to run into the captains arms, to find her and their unborn child alive- and yet, his remnants of magic still burned too bright with rage. His heart thumped against his ribcage, desperate to escape and spill it's secrets to the world. His skin was on fire as he felt his wounds knit themselves together before parting again – a typical punishment bestowed upon elves who used forbidden magic to find a means to an end. Sparks flickered at his fingertips and he knew it would not be long before his magic would explode and catastrophise the world.

He ran and ran until he found his way to an empty field, and yet his mother continued to call after him, the power of her ghostly voice forced him to slow down and listen, but alas, he could not stop running.

"Julian my boy, stop running!"

"Mother, I cannot!" He cried as he turned to face her, the elven runes turned gold against his pale skin, "Look at me! If I do not expel this magic, then I shall surely die – you know first-hand just how cruel the universe can be when you try to protect those you love."

"But that does not mean you have to do this alone."

"I cannot do this in view of the captain, not in good conscience. She is injured, our child is in danger because of me! I did this, mother," he bellowed as he fell to his knees in the field. His hands lingered on the grass as he fought to keep his magic inside.

"Julian, if I have told you once, I have told you a thousand times – none of this was your fault. But please, allow me to help you."

"If I touch you as I am..." he said as he swallowed the lump in his throat and met his mother's eyes, "You shall cease to exist."

"I had accepted that long ago, but now because of you, I can finally rest," she explained as she took her sons hand in one of hers and placed her free hand on the grass in front of her, "Be a good husband and a good father."

"If I am half as good as you, I can die happy," he smiled sadly and squeezed his mother's hand tightly before placing his spare hand on the grass in front of him, his damp hair had started to curl at the front and stick to his forehead as the expense of his wounds made him sweat, his eyes were watery from the pain but they shone with pride as he shared one last look towards his late mother, "Are you certain this is what you want?"

"If it means that you will get to have a good life, that is full of love, happiness and adventure then I would do anything for you."

S. L. Coe

"I love you darling mother."

"And I you," she said as she pressed their joined hands onto the grass and began to whisper the Elven enchantment.

As she whispered, he cried and shouted the enchantment. The runes were stubborn as they stuck to his skin for as long as they could before they were made to turn into sparks. The sky glowed burgundy as their joint magic lit the grass and sparked against the night sky. His mind swirled with the sound of Tome's laughter, the memories of the captains suffering came to light and played on repeat like a broken record until Julian could take it no more. His body folded in on itself as he screamed like a banshee, finally allowing the past ten years of boiling rage to explode and fly far-far away from him. His mother's voice softened as she began to fade away, a soft proud smile spread across her face as she let his hand fall gently to the ground.

"Let your chaos and destruction explode," she whispered as she embraced him from behind one last time before wondering into the circle of flames that lingered on the grass around them.

And let his chaos explode he did as the Elven chant ripped itself from his throat, and all sights of the rune, the torture and the harsh memories bestowed by Tome left him.

The grass hissed and growled as the fire ran its course.

He was finally free.

And it was only when the roar of the fire died down into a low simmer, did he hear the captains voice calling to him. It was louder than he had ever known it to be, "Find me!" she bellowed, and he knew that it was just a trick of the wind but that didn't stop him from gathering all the broken pieces of himself, and running to the healers home.

***

By the time he had made it to the healers home, he was completely breathless. The sky remained a strange kind of burgundy as he knocked on the door, weak and weary. "Healer are you there? Healer!" he questioned, eager for an answer.

"Come in, come in, she has not stopped asking for you," The healer said as she opened the door and quickly ushered him in and to the centre of the room where the Captain sat on the wooden sofa with a warm tankard of sage water.

Her face was pale from the pain and the rings beneath her eyes were far darker than they had been this morning, but the fact that she was breathing was all that Julian needed to calm his nerves. He fell to his knees beside her, a gentle hand placed on her thigh as he spoke, "My love, are you all right? Did he hurt you?"

"I will be okay in time," She sighed as she looked at him full of love, although worry soon began to fill her eyes as she caught sight of his wounds, "But it looks like you've been to hell and back, are you all right? Are you safe now?"

"It's only a surface wound," he said as he attempted to dismiss her worry, "It shall pass in time, and I will heal – although my magic will not return."

"You lost your magic?" The Captain questioned as she took him by the hand and invited him to sit beside her with a muttered apology for hurting his hands.

"I did. That is why it took me so long to come to you, and trust me my love, I wanted to come and find you as soon as I left the cavern – do remind me to talk to Thorian, I owe him an apology – but the magic within my system was going to kill me if I did not expel it. And thus, my mother and I found refuge in a nearby farm – she is...she is no longer on this plane because of me, but alas, I can no longer perform any kind of magic." He sighed and held his hand up to reveal the only rune that remined – and it was the elven rune for love, eternal – "This is the only thing that remains, but after an hour has passed that too will fade. Willow, I am sorry I sent you away...I..."

"My love, it is okay. If the situations were swapped, I would have gladly done the same. You did what you thought was best, and in doing so, you saved my life."

"And our daughter? Does she live?" he questioned as fearful tears pricked his eyes, his voice wobbled as he met her eyes, "Please- "

"She is very much alive," she smiled as she placed his hand onto her stomach, and whilst there was no heartbeat to be found yet, they could feel the life force pulsing through her and into the world.

"Oh thank the gods," he sighed as he embraced the captain in a warm hug, he didn't care if he suffered another burn thanks to the hot sage water, he just wanted to hold her in his arms, "I was petrified that I had cost you and her your lives."

"And if you did, I would not have blamed you," she said as she put her tankard aside and wrapped her arms around the bard. She couldn't help but bury her head in the crook of his neck as she ran small circles over his back, careful to find his fresh wounds. He squeezed her in return and placed a quick and gentle kiss to her cheek.

"I promise you, once we are free of this Island I shall build us a house, free from danger. I know we have the ship, but I swear to you Miss Willow Embers, I will always keep you safe," he whispered into her hair as he kept her close.

"And I promise you, that I will not be going anywhere, regardless of what happens in this lifetime, I shall remain by your side. That much I am certain," she smiled against his neck, "And I look forward to being your wife."

"And I your husband, and I am sorry that I was not more romantic in our proposal, I was just terrified that

I would never get a chance to ask you," he apologized as he pulled back and placed a kiss onto her forehead.

"Well maybe, you'll just have to ask me again when you have the ring," she said, almost playfully as she pulled him into a soft kiss. She couldn't help but brush his damp hair from his face and run her hands along his smooth jaw.

"I will do that as soon as it arrives," he smiled, full of love and life as he cupped her face and poured every ounce of love he had for her into his kiss.

It was with a giggle that the captain pulled away, "I think we have an audience," she said as she pointed to the window behind him where the majority of their crew and the elven child stood, smiling and full of pride.

"It would appear so, healer, could we invite them in?" he said as he sat beside the captain and finally allowed the healer to look over his wounds.

"Of course, you two are going to be the death of me," she laughed as she gave the signal for the crew to come in.

The Elven child and Thorian were the first to approach.

"Thorian, I am so sorry for snapping at you and pushing you away earlier, it was not right and I assure you that it will not happen again. I prom-"

"Bard, please stop apologizing. I'm not mad at ya, I never was. I was just bloody worried, all I hear is you screaming, captain-less, and then I see you dash for the exit. I just wished to know you were okay."

"Thank you Thorian, I promise you, I shall be – ow-okay," he said as he felt the healer pull his bandages on his hands tighter.

"I know you will, the pair of you are terrible you know that," he jested, and smiled at the couple.

"You're not much better," Julian playfully chided and sent him a wink and nodded towards Juliet.

"Bard!"

"Thorian!"

"We have much to discuss tonight, but first I believe the little one wanted to say something," he said as he moved to the side to allow the small elven child to run forward.

"Mr. Julian?" she spoke as she pointed to her ears and nodded – indicating that her hearing had returned.

"Yes my dear?"

"Thank you, for saving me."

"It was my pleasure, what is your name?"

"Nixie Bell," she said as she held her hand out to him.

Julian raised an eyebrow as he held his freehand out to her, unsure of what to expect. And within her hand, she held the ring that he had purchased for the captain.

"I think you should give it to the pretty captain."

"I think you are right, Nixie," he smiled as he took it gently in his hands, and turned to the captain – who was already smiling lovingly at the sight of her lover and the elven child – "My darling Willow, you have stood by my side through thick and thin. Without you, I would not have escaped that bandit ship, nor would I be alive today. And despite everything that stands against us, I could not imagine anyone else who fills my heart with as much love and confidence as you, and so with all the hope in the world, I ask you my darling Captain Willow, will you do me the greatest honour of being my wife?"

"Oh Julian, I will! I will!" she beamed and placed a joyfully, although slightly ill placed kiss onto his lips, and held her shaking hand out for the ring. And with shaking hands of his own, he placed the thick silver ring that was engraved with a lute and an anchor onto her ring finger.

"You have made me the happiest man in the world!" He cried as he pressed a kiss to her ring finger.

"And you me the happiest woman!" she beamed back, and with that the crew and the healer, broke out into a loud cheer, the clapped, they whistled, they cried and got ready to celebrate the new beginning.

The Bard and His Captain book 1: Damn Those Gods
Inkpot

"We shall find ourselves at the tavern tonight, and in the morning we shall make our way to Pixie Isle!"

"Aye! Aye!"

Chapter 21: I see the tavern burning bright into the bleak night.

When they sat in the tavern that night, it was unnaturally quiet spare for the soft strumming of Julian's lute. The tavern regulars had long departed their usual spots and either headed to bed or prepared to leave the isle. The bards skin stung as the last rune was leaving him, but he ignored it as he laid his head in the captains lap and enjoyed the feel of her fingers combing through his hair.

"It's too quiet," Thorian said as he looked up from his tankard and wrapped an arm around Juliet.

"I agree. Where is everyone? Surely, they haven't left yet?" Juliet questioned as she looked around the tavern, that within the space of an hour, already felt far smaller than it had when they arrived only five weeks ago. Dust was beginning to collect on the floor, and spiders happily prepared their home for the coming autumn.

"Do you think that is our sign to leave?" Julian said as he sat up with his lute placed between his legs.

"I do not believe we are far off overstaying our welcome," The Captain said as she looked towards the bar where the tavern-maid had just slammed down a closed sign and shoved the last four tankards full of ale towards the end of the bar with a harsh jolt of her head. An indication to drink up and get out or drink up and retreat to bed, lest they wish to pay their weight in gold.

"I suppose we best drink up and regroup in the morning," Julian said as he stood from the table and threw his lute over his shoulder. His skin was still paler than usual from the effects of the healers magic – he knew it would not be long before his elven blood rejected it.

"Won't you play us a song?" Thorian asked as he too stood and walked towards the stairs.

"Not tonight, I do not have the energy for a great performance. But once my next ballad has been composed, I shall be sure to put on a great performance, just for the crew."

"I shall hold you to that bard, come let us rest." The captain said as she took his hand and lead the way up the stairs, more than eager to fall into sleeps tender embrace.

"As you wish, my lady," he smiled and gave her hand a squeeze as everyone retreated up the stairs and bid the tavern-maid goodnight.

When they finally got to the stage, Julian's breath caught in his throat and he couldn't help but cough and splutter into the sleeve of his cream poet shirt. A small curse left his lips when he looked down at his cuff and saw the tale-tale sign of magic rejection, his blackened elven blood had betrayed him once again.

"Bard, are you alright?"

"Hmm? Oh yes, yes, I am perfectly fine," he said as he quickly wiped his lips with the cuff of his sleeve just in case any of his blood has slipped out of his mouth and down his chin.

"You're bleeding. Captain, tell him he is not okay."

"Thorian, I promise this is normal," the bard tried and failed to defend himself against Thorin's worry.

"Thorian, Juliet, I shall deal with this tonight. Be at the ship for eight AM sharp tomorrow morn," She said as she bid them good night and pushed the bard into their room, locking the door to prevent from any wandering eyes or ears. "What is going on? I thought you said you were okay."

"Willow, I am fine. It is just a process that us elven folk go through when we lose all of our magic. We...I cannot...my body cannot absorb the magic the healer used to heal my internal wounds – and unfortunately that blood has to go somewhere, and that place it has chosen is out of my mouth," he said as he sat on the bed and placed his hands on the captains hips – for she stood before him, between his legs. He met her eyes, and gave her an encouraging smile while he kept his eyes soft and full of love, even though he could not read her facial expression.

Her breath came out in a shudder as she felt a single cold tear slip down her cheek, "Are you going to live? Will you heal from all of this?" she questioned and forced her voice not to wobble and her legs to hold her as she looked over the bruises that littered the face of the man she loved.

"I promise you; I shall live until I am the ripe old age of 100. Us elven folk have a way of surviving, and it is in situations like this it is not the prettiest," he said as he took one of her hands in his and drew several small non-sensical patterns across her skin. "Look at me, please."

"I'm sorry Julian," she whispered as she met his eyes, and allowed for all of her shields to come crumbling down onto the ground until she couldn't hold it any longer, "If we never had have met, you would not have been in this situation."

"My lady, even if we had not met, he would have come for me one way or another. Please believe me when I say this, I have absolutely no regrets in meeting you. If I did, I would not have placed that ring upon your finger," he said as he laid back on the bed and brought her with him, so that she laid with her head on his chest. "So tell me, what is it that truly is scaring you?"

"It was something my mother said...." She whispered, a whimper lingering in her throat as she clutched to the bards stained shirt.

"I am listening," he said as he ran his hands through her hair and placed a gentle kiss onto her forehead.

"She said that my curse, would not end with me. That even if I did manage to find a cure for it, it would only be temporary, I am destined for death – and there are only two moons left until I am said to meet my end, which means..."

"That our..."

"Yes, if I had known, I would have never..." she blubbered as she clung to him and allowed for her tears to flow freely through her shaking body.

"My love, perhaps your mother was wrong," he said as he gazed towards the window, tears shimmered in his own eyes as he spotted the moon sat at her apex, full and bright. "It is a full moon tonight."

"And what of it?"

"Look at your hands, they are still covered with skin. Your body has not yet betrayed you, so perhaps, perhaps it was a strange tale that your mother heard. Perhaps she lied to you."

"I wouldn't put it past her..." she whispered as she looked towards her hands and then out of the window, and saw that he was right.

"Exactly. Come rest for tonight, it has been a long and excruciating day and fretting tonight will not make us any better," he said as he pulled the covers out from beneath them and wrapped it around the two of them. "We shall discuss this in the morning, you need to sleep."

"As do you, you are more injured than me."

"Maybe so," he smiled softly and pressed a gentle kiss onto the captains lips, and she returned it in kind, but beneath the loving kiss, their remained an unspoken yet recognised sadness that would soon come to its apex. "Goodnight, my captain."

"Goodnight, my bard."

***

The morning light had come, broke, and gone all in one as the captain and her bard tossed and turned in their shared bed. They had tried everything to exhaust themselves, up to and including sex – and whilst it was great to begin with, they did not have the energy to bring it to anything more than heavy petting – and thus they settled for cuddling instead.

His fingers were light as they drifted through her messy golden brown hair, and his voice was soft like the summer rain as he spoke. "My love, what is keeping you from sleep?"

"Nothing feels right," she muttered as she ran her hands through his soft chest hair, "I cannot help but think that danger is rapidly approaching."

"You are not the only one," he sighed with a heavy chest and turned his gaze towards the ceiling, "I suspect there is one person to blame for this feeling, and it's not one I am fond of."

"Nor I, but the more I look towards the window, the stranger the sun becomes. Have you ever known it to be so orange?"

"Only when there is fire on the horizon," he muttered, his eyes wide with panic as he slowly untangled himself from the captain and strode towards the window. A shuddered sigh left his lips as he looked out of the window and towards the right of the bay where he could see the flames of the mages fire licking at the invisible barrier that stood between Pixie Isle and the rest of the world. He turned to the captain, his eyes still wide and his breath caught in his throat, "My love, I need to borrow your ship! Pixie Isle is under attack and there is nothing I can do about it from where I stand now. Please allow me to take her, I promise you I will return her in great condition-"

And yet before Julian could finish his plea, the captain was out of bed and dressed with his clothes in hand, "Put those on, I am coming with you. Sleep and chaos can wait for us." She said as she passed him the pile of clothes and took a look out of the window. She was horrified to say the least, and she knew in that moment that she had no other choice but to raise the alarm and gather every one of her crew in case this was a sign of war.

And in their hearts of hearts they knew that this war would not be one that is so easily won nor fought.

Chapter 22: A war upon my ship and a battle upon Pixie Isle.

As they sailed across the harsh Dracondian sea, the flames merely licked at the magical barrier that was struggling to protect the Isle from harm. And yet as the ship began to dock, the flames seemed to roar with excitement and make their way to the tavern. The ship had barely made port when Julian threw his legs over the side of the ship and proceeded to jump off.

His blood boiled within him and his heart ached as the sky was painted orange and the grass that once aided the blessing of the isle, was scorched to the point of ash. Thousands of elven bodies laid slain, pissed on and branded with the elven word for traitor across their forehead so they would never know what it is like to rest.

"Tell me king Julian, does this please you? Does seeing the bodies of your people slain bring you pleasure?" Ethra spat as they emerged from the flames, and elven head in hand – Ethra had never been one to like those of elven blood, but she learnt to play the part spectacularly well, "Because when you left us to gallivant off on your adventure, our land was left without a ruler! I tried to warn you about what Tome's magic would do, and yet it was you who refused to listen!"

"No! You do not get to pin this on me. It is because of you Ethra, that Tome was able to infiltrate the castle. He should have never been able to step foot onto Pixie Isle, let a known make his way into the castle. You gave him access. You caused this."

"I -"

"Do you seriously believe that lying to me is your smartest move right now? Because I swear to you Ethra, if you lie to me again, every restraint I have will snap, and you will not escape with your life. The captain and I will make sure of it." Julian hissed as he stalked towards Ethra, his sword drawn at his side and his eyes full of rage. The captain followed close behind and whilst her blood boiled for Julian, the sheer power that radiated from his anger sent a shiver of almost fear down her spine.

"But I am not afraid of you nor her. What are you really going to do. Torture me? Make me wish I was dead? Because let me tell you something, *bard*, your worst nightmare is only just beginning, give it another evening and your hell will become your reality."

"Perhaps it shall, or perhaps I should feed you to the sirens and allow them to do with you what they will, and when your body finally emerges to the shore I will rip off your head and place it upon a spike for all to see. This is what happens to traitors," he spat as he tossed his sword to the ground, his whole body trembled with anger as he shoved Ethra to the floor – gladly ignoring her pleas.

"Allow me," the Captain spoke as she picked his sword up off of the ground and dragged it down the traitors back and allowed single drop of poisoned magic to roll down the blade and into the incision before chucking the sword aside and tying the traitors hands behind their back, "Say hello to the devil for me," she hissed in Ethra's ear as she hauled them to her feet and shoved them towards her crew, who were already lying in wait.

"Captain..." Julian whispered her title as he looked at her, his eyes shined against the harsh sun and filled with fear, "I am losing myself to this."

"Julian, you are not the monster you believe yourself to be. You are trying to protect your people, your home, you are grieving and that is okay, but what is not. Is blaming yourself for the destruction before us."

"But I have killed people! That was not me, I...I was just a simple bard not so long ago, and now I have ended the lives of so many and for what?"

"And you have created lives and saved many more than you have ended" The Captain said as she took his hands in hers and sat him down on a fallen tree whilst she simply kneeled before him.

"My love, I thank you for your optimism, but I struggle to understand how you can bring yourself to love me. For my heart and all that I am lies with you, and I will love you until the end of my days and even after that, but how can you love me – a murderous king," his title

S. L. Coe

felt like acid against his tongue, and his stomach turned as he thought about his future as a ruler – it was not one that he had dreamed of, nor one that he wished to have any part in.

"Because I have seen you at your worst, I have seen you in your moment of sickness. Hell, I have seen you upon the brink of death and in every moment of sadness, I have recalled those of unbridled happiness – and I have fallen in love with you ever since our first night in that tavern. You are not unlovable; I know at least half of my crew love you and the other half are probably in love with you. Okay? So look at me and please believe me when I say this I will never stop loving you."

"Nor I you, I just wish that life could return to how it was," he sighed as he stood and brought her up with him.

"And they will as soon as this war is over, I promise you that. I promise that the next time we make land, you are free to give the performance of your life at a tavern of your choosing," she smiled softly and pulled the bard into a warm and loving embrace.

He couldn't help but bury his head in the crook of her neck and hold her so close that he was almost afraid to let go. "And I will do it in your honour," he said, his voice soft and gentle as he brushed a stray strand of hair from his lovers face, and met her eyes which deeply mirrored her affection, "You are my muse."

"And you are mine," she said as she stood on her tiptoes and placed a long loving kiss onto the bard's lips, which he responded to in kind.

He didn't know whether this kiss would be his last, or if there was more to come but one thing he was certain off, was that the world would know of his captain and he would return to the journey of being a bard again. And everything in the world would be right.

Chapter 23: Take me to war, honey, I dare

you.

Or so the bard thought. But his thoughts could not be further from reality as he pounded on what was left of the gold castle door. He demanded to know what had sparked this spiteful culling. He demanded answers. He demanded justice. And yet the windows were covered in a thick black ink – a tell-tale sign that the elves had given up their fight and had decided to end it once and for all – and the birds that once sang upon the castle walls fell silent.

The whole world did not move for a solid minute.

The captain eyed the castle with a lump in her throat and regretful tears in her eyes as she averted her gaze and allowed Julian to silently grieve, or rather simmer in anger as he turned around and faced the forest.

"NICODEMUS!" His ex-bed fellows name tore from his throat as he stormed towards the forest and into the vampires den.

"Wait Julian! You said it yourself, a vampire's bite is fatal to you," the captain said as she ran to stand in front of her and placed a gentle hand on his chest to keep him from moving any further. "And believe me my love, I know that you are beyond furious, but you do not have any potions that will prevent you from being killed by them, and if Ethra has turned on us what is to say they will not do the same."

"Because Anya would not allow him to live for another second if he so much as harmed us," Julian said as he took her hand in his own and lead the way into the deep dark forest, unsure of what lied ahead, "And if he so much as flashed his fangs at you, I would stand in his way."

"And let yourself die?"

"To protect you? Yes," he said with a fierce determination and held one finger up to silence her protest, "My darling, you know I am not going anywhere."

"The war would suggest otherwise," she muttered, gave his hand a squeeze and pressed herself against his arm in an effort to conserve heat and hide her face from him.

"Oh Willow my love, this is not the first war I have seen and it will probably not be the last. Most humans hate us elves and that is part of the reason as to why I was put on that bandits ship almost a year ago. But I promise regardless of what happens, I will follow you until my end of days. And perhaps even after then," he smiled softly and lifted his arm so that he could pull her into a gentle embrace, and easily pull her away from the danger that lurked within those woods.

"But what if I have to go down with the ship?"

"Then by the gods in the sky and the devils that lurk in the eyes of drunken men, I will follow you down there," he all but hissed and whilst his words were determined, his voice was thick with concealed fury. Not at her, but the vicious sea, which he was slowly coming to loathe. He kept his eyes on their path and remained quiet as they walked ahead. He knew it was a conversation that they needed to have, he knew there was words that had to be said regardless of how much it would hurt, and yet he could not bring himself to breathe life into those said words.

Now was not the time nor was it the place, as Nicodemus's name tore from his throat again.

And yet, the shadows merely quivered in fear.

***

But that did not stop Julian as he wondered into the centre of the woods and sat himself down on a fallen tree stump before pulling his lute round to his front and kept a careful eye on the captain, who gladly confirmed that she felt safe in his presence. His fingers stung as he strummed the lute, and he was certain they would bleed all over the string – just another symptom of magic rejection – but for once, it worked in his favour as Nicodemus came out of the shadows. His crimson eyes glowed against his dark skin, and his fangs were practically dripping with venom as he stalked towards the bard and his captain.

"Julian watch out!" The Captain cried as the vampire attempted to lunge for Julian.

And yet Julian just stared blankly ahead as his gaze met the red oak dagger that was protruding from his ex-bed fellow and best friends chest. "Who did this to you?" Julian questioned as he pushed the captain behind him and held the vampire at an arms distance.

"Julian?" The vampire hissed through a pained gasp. He could barely see through the pain, but regardless of where he was, he would know the bards voice.

"It's me. You're safe now. The captain is here too, but pixie isle is under attack. Tell me, who hurt you?"

"You do not wish to know..." Nicodemus sighed as he stepped away from the bard and placed a hand over his mouth in order to stop himself from retching at the scent of elven blood, "I'm sorry Julian, but your blood absolutely reeks of magic rejection."

"I know, I lost all of my magic during the battle with Tome...and that is more than likely half of the reason Ethra wished to punish me," Julian said and threw his arms up in frustration as he made his way towards the forests opening.

And whilst the vampire held onto his supernatural speed, the stake in his chest slowed him significantly. His blood dripped onto the forest floor and in the droplets place – deadly nightshade grew. "Wait! BARD FOR ALL THAT IS HOLY STAND STILL!" the vampire growled and stormed towards the bard. The bards blood ran cold as he stopped in his tracks. "What do you mean you had a battle with Tome? He was just proclaiming his plan to rule Draconda not even an hour ago!"

"You mean he is still alive, after everything he has done. After the beatings I inflicted; he still has the audacity to breathe!" Julian growled, his blood boiled and the runes that had once left his skin slowly crept back to their rightful place. "And it is because of him that Ethra has defiled my people and slain countless others. And it is because of that retched bitch that I cannot find my sister anywhere."

"Oh god, if Ethra knows Tome is alive that means..." The captain said as she looked out of the forest opening and towards her ship. Her heart sank for her crew, for she knew what lied in wait. She knew that history was bound to repeat itself, and unfortunately, there was nothing that she could do to stop it. "Fuck this, we cannot just stand around and mope. And whilst I would love to scream at the world with you, it will get us nowhere. We cannot allow for these pitiful pieces of shit to win the war."

"Quite right my dear, I am coming with you."

"But you'll die!" Julian said as he pointed to the orange sun and gestured to the fact that Nicodemus was essentially running on fumes.

"I am a dead man already. Let me do this as my final wish." He said and looked between the bard and the captain, "Captain, please talk some sense into your fiancée."

"Julian, he might be right…I know you are scared for the future and I am too, but the longer we hide out in the woods, the more likely it becomes that elven lives are put on the line."

"But I cannot have any more blood on my hands, especially not yours nor Nicodemus's' nor Anya's! For without the three of you I am nothing and my reputation shall spiral down the drain."

"Julian listen to me." The captain said as she stood on her tiptoes and cupped his face, "Nicodemus has chosen his fate. He has decided that he wants to ally with us and free the land of pain. And my crew are willing to do just the same. Allow us in, allow us to fight in this war. The sooner it is over, the sooner we can return to life as we know it. We could even sail far from here and you could re-build your reputation as a bard, and forget the title of king. So please, my love, my light, allow yourself to be helped and for Christ sakes do not allow yourself to fight this war alone."

"And what happens if you die?" he whispered as he gently rested his forehead on hers and placed his hands over hers.

"Then I will die knowing that I have been loved. And that is not something that I acknowledge easily," she chuckled despite the circumstances.

"If that is your choice then so be it, I shall honour it, and yours too, Nicodemus."

"I wondered how long it would take for you to come around, bard," Nicodemus chimed in with an amused smile as he watched the two lovebirds come apart and offer their hands to him.

"Did you want me to pull that stake out?" Julian half jested half questioned as he raised a teasing eyebrow.

"Only if you're gentle."

"Oh I always am!"

"AGHHHHHH! YOU CALL THAT *FUCKING GENTLE!*"

Chapter 24: Sail gently into the reapers

waters dear sister!

Thunder clapped across the sky in time to the sound of swords clashing against swords, and arrows flying overhead. No one sang the bards song and the once gentle and majestic isle was a bloodbath of fallen elves, orcs and the ash piles of cremated vampires. The tavern itself still stood, but barely as flames licked at the door.

Julian felt his heart drop in his stomach as the flames erupted in a ball of sparks and made their way into the tavern. With wide eyes and a pounding in his chest and ran to the door, desperate to find away in "ANYA!! ANYA!" he cried as he kicked and tried to barge the door open. But it was futile, the magic that protected the tavern was putting up a fight, and he would not emerge victorious.

"Is she in there?" The captain questioned, raising her voice over the roar of the flames as she ran around to the side of the tavern to look in the window.

"I do not know, but I have not seen her. Shit!" he cursed as he flicked the flame off of his shirt and ran around the back of the tavern, stripping himself of his lute and digging in his satchel for any potion that could potentially heal his sister. "Leave me and find us a mage!"

"Julian?"

"Nicodemus. Listen to me, she is my sister, if anyone is going to sit with her whilst death draws near, it is me. Now take the captain and my lute and go!" He hissed and flung the hatch door open and began to descend the ladder without checking to see if Nicodemus and the captain had left. His eyes took a while to adjust to the darkness, but amongst it, he could hear the pained cry of his sister.

"ANYA! I can't see anything in here, where are you?"

"What are you doing here?" Anya questioned as she gasped for air and tried to push the fallen beam off of her ribcage.

"Me? What about you, you should have fled the isle at the first sight of danger."

"And leave the tavern to die? To let Ethra kill my patrons? There is not a chance in hell I would allow that to happen."

"It already has" he sighed as he followed her voice and used the last dreg of magic to illuminate the room. Bile rose in his throat as he saw the way Anya's leg had been broke and bent in the wrong direction, one of her horns was snapped and placed through her left hand. "Who did this to you?"

"Who do you think?"

"I will kill her!" he growled, and placed his hand underneath the beam, far more than ready to push it off of her.

"Julian, your bleeding...no..."

"Shh, we'll worry about me later. We need to save you."

"Does the captain know that you're dying?"

"No. And she's not going to."

"But Julian, if she is to be your wife and the mother of your child, then she has a right to know. Why haven't you told her?"

"Because she plans to go down with the ship!" he snapped as he pushed all of his strength into the beam and even then it only raised a couple of inches.

Anya's words died on her tongue as she watched hurtful tears pool in the bards eyes. And in that moment she knew he was on the verge of breaking, and death would not be far behind. "Every good captain should."

"It does not mean that she has to! She may be a great captain, but she is far more than that to me – to everyone – now, she cannot just go down with the ship and expect everything to be okay."

"Julian, my darling brother, that is pa-" she gasped for air as she tried and failed to pull herself out of the small gap between the floor and the beam, "part of the pirates code...it was inevitable."

"I- I...I cannot lose her again" he whispered, his voice thick with tears as his hands shook against the beam, "Come on!"

"Julian...I can't move. I'm trapped...you have to let me go," she sighed as she allowed herself to lay still on the sodden wood floor beneath her. Every ounce of pain washed over her face and she knew that she would not be long for this world.

"No. Anya, please, do not give up on this. Look at me, okay open your eyes, please," he begged as he knelt before her and gently cupped her face to keep her gaze focused in on him. "You remember when we were kids, before everything went to hell, we used to run along the top of the castle walls, laughing like loons until one of us fell in and we had to run to the outside to save the other. Yes?"

"Yeah..."

"That's what I'm doing now, okay, I am coming to scoop you up and we'll get on the captains ship and we'll find a mage...and...and they will heal you, okay? Ju – just keep your eyes on me okay,"

She leant into his hand and closed her eyes, "Brother, if I had the strength I would fight to be here with you, but I have fought my battle. Just promise me one thing?"

"Anything," he said as he looked to the ceiling in hopes of keeping the remainder of his tears at bay, but it was futile as they streamed down his cheeks.

"Promise me, that you will be a great father to your child, no matter what happens between you and the captain, you will not allow your child to live through the same events we did," she sobbed as she reached for his hand and squeezed it, struggling to hold on.

"I promise you; I will do far more than that. our child will be the most loved child in all of Draconda, and I will ensure that my wife knows that she is loved. And that you are alive and well!"

"Julian, you know better than to lie to the dying."

"Anya..."

"Please, I just need the pain to be gone. Please just say what needs to be said," she begged as a wave of pain tore through her like a red hot sword.

"I cannot sentence you to death."

"I am already sentenced. You are the only one who can deliver me to him safely."

"But..."

"Julian, please. It hurts!"

"I am sorry I did not get here quicker," he cried as he bent down and embraced his sister, his voice was gentle and thick with unshed tears as he whispered *'Sail safely into deaths tender care. May he great you with kindness, and may your pain run from thee. May you be met with everything that you wished you had. And now I shall leave you to sail safely into the reapers waters'.*

"Thank...you..." she managed to whisper as her eyes slipped shut and she fell limp within his arms.

In one breath, everything he knew, everything he had considered safe and kind, slipped from his embrace and his entire body ached from the inside out. By gods he wanted to scream at the world, to rip his heart out and scream 'Is this suffering enough? Does this please you?'.

A stuttering of no's was all that left his lips as the flames roared at the door, more than ready to take Anya to death's sweet embrace.

"WILLOW!!" he screamed as he clutched at his sisters corpse in a futile attempt to free her. He knew it was useless but he couldn't stop himself from trying, "WILLOW!!"

"JULIAN!" The captain called back as she clambered down the ladder and round to where her fiancée sat, broken. "Oh gods...is she?"

"She's gone. She made me say the elven prayer. I...I cannot bring her back, even if I wanted to, the gods would defy me to keep her. I...I am worse than Ethra."

"No you are not," she said as she kneeled beside him and wrapped her arms around him. "This was not your fault, Anya held on for you. She wanted you to be the one she saw before she passed, please my love, do not blame yourself for any of this."

"But-"

"Shh my love," she said as she pressed a quick and gentle kiss to his lips before pressing one to his sweat covered forehead. "Right now is not the time to be choosing faults. Your feelings are valid, but my love, this was not you're doing."

"Are you really going to go down with your ship?" he whispered as he pressed his forehead to the captains, the timing was awful, but he was not one to have perfect timing anyway. If he was going to live with and love the captain for the rest of his days, he needed to know.

"I will. It is my code and it is my punishment," she said as she ran her fingers gently through his matted locks.

"Allow me to come with you."

"What about the crew, they'll need a captain."

"Then allow Thorian, or Juliet or hell even John to do it. But please do not make me live a life without you in it."

"I shan't," she said softly and took his hand in hers. "We need to go before the flames choose to take us as its next victim."

"I do not want to leave her, not like this."

"Anya would want to stay with the tavern." But no sooner had the words left the captains mouth, did the flames burst through the door and spark as the engulfed Anya's body, and thus left the bard without choice.

He screamed after his sister, but the captain pulled him towards the ladder and forced him to climb.

He had seen enough death for one day.

And Anya had gotten to live the life that she had wished for.

Chapter 25: If I had to choose a day to lose you, I suppose today is better than none.

"No stop, please, I beg of you! She is with child, for Christ sake do not end two lives for the sake of one. Allow me to take her place! Kill me instead!" Julian cried as he broke free of his bonds and ran to stand in front of the heavily pregnant captain.

His heart pounded against his ribcage as he saw blood pool at the captains feet. "No..."

"I'm so sorry, Julian" she sobbed as she clung to her stomach and felt the live within her fade.

Her heart tore in two as she watched the blade come down and slash across the bards chest.

He was for deaths harsh shore, and their future would die with her as that same tainted sword sliced straight through her stomach and to her core.

And whilst she knew her pregnancy may never come to term; she did not think it would end like this.

A brutal bloodbath.

***

S. L. Coe

Her blood curdling screams filled the entirety of their shared bedroom as thunder cracked like a whip against the sky and the waves slapped the side of the ship.

"Hey, Captain. Wake up! Wake up! It's just a dream!" The Bard whispered as he held his lover close and gently shook her awake.

She didn't want to open her eyes; she didn't want to face the reality that awaited her. But the bards voice was gentle as he pressed a comforting kiss to her forehead, "Willow my love, you are safe now. Do not panic, I will not let any harm come to you. Just open your eyes for me"

"But you're dead..."

"My love, I can assure you that is very much not the case," he said as he took her hand in his and placed it over his heart, allowing her to feel the warmth in his chest and the slightly increased rhythm of his heart. "What happened my love?"

"They killed her. They killed you..."

"Who did?"

"Tome and Ethra" she cried as she wrapped her arms around the bard and sobbed into his chest, unable to keep her confident persona up any longer. "They're playing with my memories. They're trapped in my dreams and they won't leave me be! I don't ever want to sleep again. What if – what if I dream about that again?"

"Then I will find a way to enter your dreams and keep them at bay," he promised as he sat up in the bed and brought her with him. With all of his strength he pulled her to sit in his lap, silk covers and all, so that her head could rest against his chest. "They are just dreams my dear, and in this world they cannot harm you, nor her."

"But what if you're wrong?" she sniffled as she finally found the courage to look up at him with tear filled eyes.

"Then I will face the consequences of my actions when the time is right. Until that point, I choose to focus in on what positives we have on our side at this current time," he said as he placed a gentle hand on the captains growing bump. Twelve weeks had passed since the battle of Pixie Isle, and with every day that past the bond that the three of them shared grew ever stronger – despite the symptoms. "And she is still alive and well. I promised my dear sister that I would build a life for us, and that is what I intend to do, okay? So you shall always be safe."

"Have I told you I love you today?" she smiled through her tears and placed a gentle hand over his.

"A thousand times today, but I shall gladly hear it a thousand times more. For I burn for you my dear sweet lady," he smiled softly and pressed her kiss to her temple before brushing a stray strand of hair behind her ear, "Have you had these nightmares before?"

"Never this vivid," she admitted as she buried her head in the bards chest and pulled the covers so that the both of them would be covered. "Usually they only come once the curse has taken effect...but if they are coming this early, it means..."

"I know," The bard whispered in almost silent acknowledgement. "How many moons do you think we have left?"

"One if we are lucky and if not then Ethra will find a way to punish us for taking her hostage."

"I swear when we next make land I will find the nearest Oubliette and shove her down it." He groaned.

The captain couldn't help but laugh as she watched his eyebrow twitch in irritation.

A playful smirk danced across his lips as he turned his head towards her, "What is so funny?"

"Your eyebrow is twitching like Thorian when he's had one too many eagle – meads down at the Krakens Head," she giggled and placed her fingers over it to keep it in place.

"My lady has anyone told you, that you are beyond adorable?" he laughed softly and took her hand in his before pressing a kiss onto her knuckles.

"Well my good sir, I am proud to admit that you are the first."

"Really?"

"Are you surprised?" she teased as she ran her hands through his hair and toyed with the curls that were beginning to settle on his forehead.

"My darling Willow, you are truly something special, and if the people who came before me could not see it, then they must be blind or stupid, or they just simply do not get to be as lucky as me," he said softly as he kissed her lovingly and ran his fingers along her jaw, "I cannot wait to marry you."

"Nor I you," she said as she smiled into the kiss, "I suppose going back to sleep would be a waste of time now."

"Are you sure you do not wish to rest a little longer?"

"It would not be a peaceful sleep, and we have a lot to do today."

"That's true, I suppose I should check on the villain in the brig."

"Indeed, but please Julian, as much as I wish to see her dead, we do not need any more bloodshed."

"Your wish is my command captain," he said as he stood and bowed with a flourish of his hand before he headed over to the chest of drawers and dug out a box that was covered in black and gold lace. "Here, I managed to salvage these from the kingdom before we left."

"Are they what I think they are?"

"Open it and find out."

"Julian!" She beamed as she saw a perfect replica of the gloves that she had once cherished and lost, "I thought I had lost these forever!"

"Well, I knew how important they were to you and I figured it was always a good idea, to keep a second pair handy just in case," he smiled bashfully and made his way to get dressed.

"Ah, ah, come back here," she smirked as she slipped the gloves on and beckoned him over with a curl of her finger.

"Yes, my love?"

"Allow me to thank you properly," she said as she stood on her knees and placed a passionate kiss against the bards warm lips.

***

The morning passed slowly as Julian made his descent towards the brig, dragging his feet as he went, for he knew that upon seeing Ethra's face, kindness would be the last thing on his mind. The sand that gathered at the bottom of the boat sifted through a hole in the bottom of his boots, and with his patience wearing thin (and also wanting to find a way to annoy Ethra without actually murdering them) he took his boots off and clapped them three times in tune to the same song that he, the captain and Anya, performed at the castle, before he dragged them along the bars, purposefully.

"Oi, Ethra, are you awake?" the bard called as he bashed his hand onto the bars, knowing full well that they had their head rested on them.

"I am now, you bastard" they spat as they kneeled back on their heels and watched through the bars. Their hair had become greasy and they stank to the high heavens.

"My, my, harsh words for someone who is supposedly under the captains protection," he chastised as he pulled a barrel from the discarded pile and sat on it with his legs crossed and his lute laid across them. "You know if it were not for the captain, you would be dead."

"And if it were not for Tome, you would be too so how about we skip the failed attempt at a power trip."

With that the bard rolled the sleeves of his Black poet shirt to his elbows and settled on the edge of the barrel, so that his feet just touch the floor and he brought the dagger – that the captain had gifted him many moons ago – from his boot and brought it so that it glinted between his fingers with every flick of his wrist. "Fine. Then let's play a game, I shall ask you a question, and for every time you refuse to answer me or rather lie to me, you will receive a cut until I fear you will bleed out."

"I- Yes, my lord," they said, their voice practically dripped with sarcasm as they spoke and caught onto the fact that the bard was not giving them an option to refuse.

"That is king to you. So tell me, wicked witch, how did that bastard manage to survive?"

"I do not know," they lied and hissed through their teeth as Julian's sharp blade slide down the underside of their forearm.

"Do not lie to me." He spat and glared daggers at her as he pulled his blade back through the bars, "Why must your torment the captain? She has done you no wrong and yet-"

"Oh but that is where you are wrong, she hurt me deeply when you were conked out after that little mishap with your father. I thought you would have grown used to the beatings by now, but evidently I was wrong," Ethra cooed and stuck their arm through the bars in a failed attempt to reach the bards face, but the bard caught their arm before they could and flung it into the bars so hard they were sure it crunched.

"Do not touch me."

"Oh but there is someone you wish would. What happens when the sea rises up against you and takes your precious captain from you? Oh that is what terrifies you. Well, well, well, who would have thought the infamous bard of west Draconda would succumb to such human fears."

"Fuck you," he spat as he pushed himself off of the barrel and collected up his belongings before heading towards the door.

"You know she will not care enough to come and find you once she lands in Davy jones locker!" Ethra hollered as the door slammed shut and bolted from the outside.

And whilst the bard knew their words were nothing but lies, they had managed to get in his head and he felt as though his blood was on fire.

***

Ethra's smile was giddy as they slid down the walls and used magic to heal their cuts, for they had managed to worm their way into the bard and his captains mind. A perfect place for them to lay dormant whilst Tome regathered strength and prepared to burn the world to the ground.

They knew it would only be a matter of time before the bard's patience fully snapped and he would bring an end to their life and thus, it would spark their rule over Draconda. They would no longer have to prance about pretending to be an elf and instead, they could finally embrace their true nature as incubus, hell bent on destruction.

***

"Bard!" Thorian called out as he hobbled over to the mast where the bard leant against it attempting to compose his next greatest hit.

"Thorian, are you all right?"

"I am, although I fear the weather is not on our side," he admitted just as thunder cracked through the sky and sent the rain falling onto the deck like bullets.

"Most definitely not," Julian said as he scooped up his belongings and encouraged the dwarf to move with him until they managed to find a small alcove in the side of the ship.

"We should have left by now," Thorian fretted as he toyed with the threads of his jumper.

"I know and trust me my friend, I fear that if we are to leave during the storm we may not make it to our destination by nightfall, and given that we have to pass through sirens cove, I fear it may not be in our favour."

"What does the captain say?"

"I am unsure, I have not seen her since I last spoke to Ethra earlier this morning, although if this sinking feeling is anything to go by, I feel as though Ethra may be up to her old tricks again."

"Again? Bard, why did you not tell me this morning, I could have found her a remedy."

"Because, it was not my tale to tell. And I was, I still am terrified of her dream coming true..." he sighed and stepped into the rain, just wanting to feel something other than the nagging fear that grew within his chest. The rain ran down his face and wet his shirt to the core, his long curls stuck to his face but he couldn't care less as he looked towards the captains quarters with a loving smile.

"I am certain it will not, the pirate code would not allow it," he said as he made his way over to the captains doors, "Perhaps we should ask her what our next path is?"

"Captain?" The bard called as he and Thorian knocked on the door, and whilst the response was quiet it was enough to convince them to enter.

"Hello, my love," she smiled softly as she felt Julian wrap his arm around her waist and join her as she looked over the map, "Thorian, come join us!"

"What are we looking at?"

"Our sailing path, but the more I look at it, the less likely it becomes of finding a safe path from here to the mainland," The Captain said as she dragged her hand across the map and indicated to siren's cove.

"Do you think we should undertake this voyage or would we rather wait until the morning?" Thorian piped up as he stood on a stool and ran a thin line of chalk over the path he would rather take.

"If we do not leave now, we will be stuck here until at least December. We should make sure we can set off as soon as possible."

"As long as you are sure Cap' in."

"I am. Please ready the crew Thorian, I still have some business to discuss with our bard."

"You do?"

"Indeed we do, Julian, it concerns Ethra."

"I shall leave you be," Thorian said and pushed the stool under the desk before quickly exiting the room.

"Willow, What happened?"

"It is far worse than we originally thought."

"You can say that again."

"It's far worse – oh."

Chapter 26: They always say a good captain goes down with the ship, and her bard will always be right behind her.

As the thunder crashed across the sky, fire rumbled deep within the ship, far more than ready to send the canons firing should they come into danger. The captain knew the inevitable was coming as she stood in front of the wheel, her eyes never met the bards as she stared down at the crew of 300 men and women, from every corner of Draconda. Thorian, Juliette and John stood behind the captain and at her side her most loyal lover and first mate stood, ready to serve and protect until his end of days.

But in the captains heart of hearts, she knew that she should not lie to the crew. If she were to tell the truth now, she would be at the face of mutiny again. And this time, she would be the one marooned – although if the bard had something to say about it, then it would never come to fruition.

"The crew is awaiting your instruction, my lady," the bard whispered as he bent down and placed a soft kiss onto her temple. "Trust your instinct."

The wind whipped through their hair and the picked up a deathly chill as it embraced the crew and made way for the moonlight. "I know," she whispered and held her hand out for his, which he gladly squeezed and held tight against his chest, "I just feel uneasy about the trip, and I do not wish to be marooned or mutinied."

"My darling, if that happens, I shall fight them all myself. Would you rather I give the orders?"

"No. They are my crew and this is my ship, I must be the one to do it." She said as she took a deep breath and stepped up to the railing with Julian in tow, her hair blew in the wind and her belt rattled with coins, swords and various necklaces and jewels she had stolen on their occasional pillages – long before she embarked on this life of adventure. She clapped her hands together and looked towards the crew, determined and ready for a fight, "Listen up! This voyage will be dangerous, and there is no denying that, but it is important that we stick together during this trying trip. We are too pass through siren's cove, protect yourself and do not talk to any siren's we pass. We remember what happened when Scoundrel sailed with us. Let us not repeat our mistakes. Anyone who wishes to not take part in this voyage, please find your way off of my ship, and do not expect to return to it. Am I clear?"

"Aye!" Came the cry of 250 crew members, who all glared daggers at the 50 that chose to abandon the captain in this difficult passage, they threw hurtful comments of 'Coward! Traitor! Mutineer!' at those that left but they were quickly hushed by the captain who called above their voices.

"Leave the traitors be, raise the anchor! We must be a way! Take your positions and ready your arms, we leave NOW!" she cried and made her way behind the wheel. Her gaze drifted over to the bard who watched her with a proud smile and softened gaze. "What?"

"Nothing, I've just never been more proud of you then I have in this moment. You were brilliant up there, and I cannot wait to see you in action during future voyages!"

"You flatter me far too much, my love," she smiled softly and span the wheel so the ship would begin to turn out of port and towards the deeper waters that would take them through the opening of sirens cove.

"Nonsense, my dear, you are a fine captain and even finer wife to be. Now let us sail out to sea."

"I have a feeling you're attempting to compose a song."

"There is one in the woodworks, one that I shall sing in your honour at the next tavern."

"I long to hear it."

***

The rocks beneath the sea at sirens cove were harsh and vile as they carved away at the bottom of the black Bess, and whilst she put up a good resistance, the cravings were beginning to turn into holes- holes big enough to allow a siren to make her away aboard the ship with no one being any of the wiser. The wind hissed through the rocks and sliced against the crews skin as they worked to manoeuvre the ship between the narrow mountains. The rain thudded against the wooden floor of the ship, and the lighting flashed across the sky.

They had not heard from Ethra since this morning, and yet, it was the creek and snap of metal and wood that drew the captains attention away from the path ahead, and instead focused it upon the brig.

"Julian," she said as she looked at him with wide eyes before forcing herself to focus on their journey.

"I know," was all that he muttered as he fled from her side, plucked a sword up from within the wood and ran down to the brig. "I will bring us to safety!" he called behind him, but it was futile for the sound of rain and thunder drowned his voice.

"My, my, so the bard does know how to take back control," Ethra cooed as they walked forward and dusted themselves off, a large elven rune that read Tome's name over and over again sat high upon their breastbone and made its way to their cheek.

"How did you-?"

"Escape? Oh how you underestimate me boy! You always did during your days at court so I do not know as to why I am so surprised you would do the same now."

"During my days at court, Ethra, I received beating after beating and the only person who did anything to prevent, you had slaughtered only a month ago. So forgive me Ethra, if I do not particularly expect any less from a villain such as yourself."

"Sticks and stones, king, sticks and fucking stones!" They said as they attempted to walk out of the small alcove that they made, but alas Julian's sword made it first.

"You will not be leaving this room alive, and you most certainly will not be stepping foot near my captain," he hissed as he brought his sword from the entrance to base of their throat.

"Ah but was it not your precious captain that specifically stated that you were not allowed to kill me," they tormented as they went to move the sword and yet gasped as the tip caught their skin.

"She never said I couldn't beat you into an inch of death," he spat as the lightning cracked against the sky and waves crashed into the side of the ship.

Julian could feel a pit of nausea grow in his stomach as the sirens song started to grow louder in volume, and it would not be long before the lesser of the crew were drowned and killed by those honeyed words. His eyes rolled as he tried to keep the noise at bay. But it was in that moment that he felt the cold kiss of steel against

S. L. Coe

his chest, and he knew then, in that moment, that the battle was on.

Swords clashed against swords as the ship creaked and moved harshly from side to side as the captain tried to mauver the black Bess through corners that it ought not to go down. As Julian went to raise his sword and strike a Ethra, his footwork became undone and he went hurtling into the side of the ship before meeting the floor. A rock from beneath the sea splintered the bed of the ship.

"What say you, bard, are you going to finish the job or will you always be a pitiful victim of situation?" Ethra teased maliciously as they stood above him with their sword dangling over the bards stomach.

But the bard remained quiet as water lashed at his skin, the sword he held in his left felt heavier than he had ever known it to be. But with it came an immense wave of power and he slipped from beneath his former squire and brought his sword down against theirs. He paid no mind to Ethra's words, although they cut deep, the hatred and fury that he held for them ran deeper still.

And that is when it all went to hell.

For the ship lurched forward and with it, so did the bard and his sword. The sword buried itself to the hilt inside Ethra's breast, and the bards breathe stuck in his throat as he tried to pull away from them.

But alas, it was futile for even in their dying moments Ethra's strength grew and they dug their nails under the bards skin as they pulled him down so they could whisper in his ear, "Goodluck being marooned. I hope it kills you."

And with that they shoved him to the ground and feigned death. Julian did not know where to look as he saw Ethra lying lifeless and his sword buried deep within them. He could not let the captain see this.

For if she did, then everything that they had worked towards, everything that they held dear would be for nothing.

She would hate him, or so the bard thought as he pulled his sword free and carried Ethra from the wall into her original cell.

He placed his sword beside her, a feeble attempt to make it look like the wound was self-inflicted. A smirk stayed put on the squire's semi – corpse.

"I am sorry," was all that the bard muttered before he wiped his hands on his shirt and ran out of the room and back to the captains side.

She need never know.

***

But the captain always did. She did not speak of the situation as she span the wheel and commanded that the crew let the cannons fire as they approached a ship full of sirens in disguise.

"Captain!" The bard cried above the noise of the cannons, "Are you sure this is the best course of action?"

"It is our only course," she said as she gestured to the holes already beginning to form in her ship. She held her breath as a cannon ball and chain tore through the underside of the ship, close to the brig, "If you nor I did not kill Ethra, then the cannon ball would."

"I am sorry."

"We will talk about this later. For now take control of the wheel, I need to speak to my crew."

"But I do not know how to steer a ship!"

"Then learn! Please Julian, I need to do this!" she said as she descended the staircase, her swords and trinkets clanged as she went, her hat barely stayed upon her head as she ran to the crow's nest.

"Captain?" came the question of the crew as they eyed her with a worried curiosity.

"Listen to me, you all have served me well," she said and moved so that she was out of sight of the bard. "But it appears this journey was far more dangerous than I had first anticipated...if we carry on like this..." she explained and ducked as another cannon ball tore

through the centre of the mast, "We will not make it
out alive. And so for this one day, should you wish to
flee with your lives and return to whatever is left of my
ship, please find your way to shore now."

"No Captain, if you go down, we go down." John said
from amongst the crowd, "You have served us just as
we have served you, we are your crew."

The Captain opened her mouth to speak, and yet no
words come out as lighting hit the deck, almost ready
to split the ship into as her lover almost crashed into
the rocks. There was nothing she could do to stop the
inevitable as splinters of her ship flew through the air
and tore into the sides of her crew. The siren's song
grew louder and louder as they attempted to crawl up
the side of the ship and pull her fellow pirates down
into the unforgiving sea.

As she walked forward, every step she seemed to take
was shakier than the last. The fire roared as it took the
mast in its favour and engulfed it whole.

"Captain!" The bard shouted as he reached his hand
out for her, and yet she simply shook her head. "No,
come on Willow, we cannot end our fight like this."

"We do not have any other choice Julian! My ship is in
ruin, my mast is on fire and I fear that the crew will
succumb to a watery grave," she said as she took
control of the wheel, her gaze passed to Juliette and
Thorian – who with remorseful tears in their eyes –
understood what was about to happen.

"Thank you Captain, for everything," Thorian said as he embraced the captain from behind and Juliette from the side.

"Thank you, both of you. I hope that life is kind to you, and that you, get to sail again soon," she said, and withheld a scream as her curse tried to break free from its confines.

"To the captain! To honour, and too a life well sailed!" Thorian's voice boomed as he spoke and ignited the crew with a new sense of life as he prepared to guide them off of the ship and onto the sailing boats. "Come with us bard."

"No. I am staying with the captain!" he said as he stood firmly behind her.

But again she shook her head and tore her gaze from the sea, and looked at her lover with soft tear filled eyes. "My love, you cannot. Where I am going is for me and me alone, if I were to take you down to Davy Jones' locker you would die the most painful death, and I would not be able to live with myself," she said softly and cupped the bard face, her almost skeletal thumb ran across his cheek as she allowed herself to have this one bittersweet moment of bliss before she succumbed to the underworld.

"Then let me die with you. What about...what about our baby?"

"Julian."

"No Willow, I know you are a good captain and I know this is what you must do!" he cried as a chain shot flew through the balcony of the ship and left the staircase to crumble away. "But we have more than just you or I to think about!"

"Don't you think I know that? Hell if I could avoid this situation I would. But I cannot and as such me and our child must go down with the ship, we do not have a choice."

"Let me come with you!"

"No." Was all that the captain said as she span the wheel and headed between the two enemy ships.

"I love you," he whispered as he stood behind her and pressed a kiss to her temple, almost resigning himself to the truth.

"And I love you, in time, I shall see you again, but for now...now I must do this." She said as she looked back up at him, and beckoned him towards her, "Please, let me do this, alone."

"Promise me, promise me, you will find a way to contact me," he said as he ran his hands through her hair, savouring the feeling.

"I promise you that Julian, I will never stop searching for you."

"Nor I you, and I hate that it has come to this," he admitted as he swooped down and kissed her, hard.

"Go, before another cannon ball tries to take you out!" she commanded as she placed both hands tight on the wheel and watched her crew pile into the row boats.

And yet he lingered, unwilling to leave, unwilling to abandon ship and abandon his captain. But the strength and volume of his voice was enough to convince him to leave her be.

He knew in his heart of hearts that he find her again but as he sat within the rowboat and watched the enormous jagged rock plough into the centre of the ship, he couldn't help but scream.

The Captain took her hands of the wheel as the row boats took off into the distance, she knew death was coming as the stairs crumbled away and the floor splintered piece by piece until the half on which she stood rapidly began to sink.

"CAPTAIN!!" Julian cried as he attempted to jump from his seat and swim to the ship, but he was held back by Thorian and Juliet, "LET ME GO. I NEED TO SAVE HER!"

"You can't save her; she is with Davy Jones."

"NO. I refuse to believe that," he said as hot tears streamed down his face and he continued to fight against their hold.

Lighting ripped across the sky and world roared as the rain pummelled onto the ship. The Black Bess cracked in two and exploded beneath the brig as the

Captain, who had closed her eyes and heart to the scene, went down with it, until nothing remained of the ship.

The bards entire being wanted to break in two, his heart bled for her, and his eyes saw red as he gripped the side of the rowboat, a guttural agonized scream left his throat as he watched her drown.

And in that moment he knew, he knew that he would never get too see her in the land of the living, again.

His shoulders shook with every sob and he could barely catch his breath as he saw her key float to the surface.

Julian's voice thundered against the wind as he reached towards the unforgiving sea:

"CAPTAIN!!!!"

S. L. Coe

Printed in Great Britain
by Amazon

33020907R00196